ROSE'S WORLD
Louisville, Kentucky, in 1886

HISTORY MYSTERIES FROM AMERICAN GIRL:

The Smuggler's Treasure, *by Sarah Masters Buckey*
Hoofbeats of Danger, *by Holly Hughes*
The Night Flyers, *by Elizabeth McDavid Jones*
Voices at Whisper Bend, *by Katherine Ayres*
Secrets on 26th Street, *by Elizabeth McDavid Jones*
Mystery of the Dark Tower, *by Evelyn Coleman*
Trouble at Fort La Pointe, *by Kathleen Ernst*
Under Copp's Hill, *by Katherine Ayres*
Watcher in the Piney Woods, *by Elizabeth McDavid Jones*
Shadows in the Glasshouse, *by Megan McDonald*
The Minstrel's Melody, *by Eleanora E. Tate*
Riddle of the Prairie Bride, *by Kathryn Reiss*
Enemy in the Fort, *by Sarah Masters Buckey*
Circle of Fire, *by Evelyn Coleman*
Mystery on Skull Island, *by Elizabeth McDavid Jones*
Whistler in the Dark, *by Kathleen Ernst*
Mystery at Chilkoot Pass, *by Barbara Steiner*
The Strange Case of Baby H, *by Kathryn Reiss*
Danger at the Wild West Show, *by Alison Hart*
Gangsters at the Grand Atlantic, *by Sarah Masters Buckey*

Danger at the Wild West Show

by
Alison Hart

American Girl®

Visit our Web site at **americangirl.com**

Printed in the United States of America.
03 04 05 06 07 08 RRD 10 9 8 7 6 5 4 3 2 1

History Mysteries® and American Girl®
are registered trademarks of Pleasant Company.

PERMISSIONS & PICTURE CREDITS
The following individuals and organizations have generously given permission to
reprint illustrations contained in "A Peek into the Past": p. 157—Circus World Museum,
Baraboo, WI (NL25-08-1F-1); pp. 158–159—"Marksmanship" poster, Circus World Museum,
Baraboo, WI (NL450-98-9F-1); William Cody figure, Buffalo Bill Historical Center, Cody, WY,
gift of the Coe Foundation; cowboy band, Circus World Museum, Baraboo, WI; galloping riders,
Western History Collections, University of Oklahoma; pp. 160–161—gun box, Chrysalis Images;
Annie Oakley, Bettmann/CORBIS; coin purse, National Cowgirl Museum and Hall of Fame,
Fort Worth, TX, photo by William Manns; trick rider, Glenbow Archives, Calgary, Alberta,
Canada (NA-628-4); fringed skirt, National Cowgirl Museum and Hall of Fame, Fort Worth, TX,
photo by William Manns; pp. 162–163—rider on pinto pony, Circus World Museum,
Baraboo, WI; Sitting Bull, Library of Congress; *Days of Long Ago* by Henry Farny
(1903), Buffalo Bill Historical Center, Cody, WY (6.75).

Cover and Map Illustrations: Jean-Paul Tibbles
Line Art: Greg Dearth

Library of Congress Cataloging-in-Publication Data

Hart, Alison.
Danger at the Wild West show / by Alison Hart. — 1st ed.
p. cm. — (History mysteries ; 19)
Summary: Twelve-year-old Rose sets out to prove her brother's innocence
when he is accused of shooting a politician during a Wild West show
performance in Louisville, Kentucky, in 1886.

ISBN 1-58485-718-8 — ISBN 1-58485-717-X (pbk.)
[1. Wild West shows—Fiction. 2. Trick riding—Fiction.
3. Indians of North America—Fiction. 4. Louisville (Ky.)—History—
19th century—Fiction. 5. Mystery and detective stories—Fiction.]
I. Title. II. Series.
PZ7.H256272 Dan 2003   [Fic]—dc21   2002071728

To cowgirls everywhere

TABLE OF CONTENTS

CHAPTER I
AN UNEXPECTED ENEMY

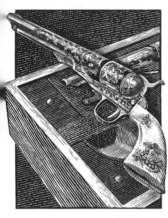

P ull!"
Twelve-year-old Rose Taylor
tripped the lever and a round clay
pigeon flew into the air. Her older
brother, Zane, eased his rifle on his
shoulder and sighted in the target.
Holding onto the top of her felt
cowboy hat, Rose tipped her head
and gazed up into the blue spring sky. The rifle cracked,
and the clay pigeon exploded.

Rose was helping her twenty-year-old brother, Zane—
Sharpshootin' Cowboy—practice his shooting act for
the famed Levi Frontier's Wild West Show. The troupe
was camped at the Louisville Jockey Club, a horse-racing
track a mile outside of Kentucky's largest city. It was a
warm Thursday afternoon in May, and Zane was practicing
in the grassy oval infield. A wide dirt track surrounded the
infield, which was edged all around by white board fencing.
Usually, hot-blooded Thoroughbreds raced around the

track. But for seven days, the Wild West troupe was using the track to perform its daring feats.

On the east side of the track, Rose could see the grandstand, with its tiers of wooden seats. To the left were the ticket wagon and concession stands, deserted for the moment. To the right of the grandstand, the wooden steward's tower jutted into the sky. From his perch high in the tower, William Pearson, the show's manager and co-owner, would announce the acts. Tonight would be the Wild West's first performance in Louisville. Rose hoped the grounds and grandstand would be swarming with eager spectators.

As Zane practiced in the infield, a group of ladies strolled around the track to watch. Their long skirts trailed in the soft dirt. Each time Zane shot, twitters and giggles rose from the group. *Silly biddies,* Rose thought impatiently. She had no time for ladies in frilly wear.

"Let's try the glass balls," Zane said. Handing Rose his rifle, he strode to the portable, velvet-draped table that Rose had set up in the infield. On top of the table was a mahogany gun box. Opening the box, he picked up one of his prized Colt revolvers and shined it with a soft cloth. But his blue eyes were on the ladies. One lagged behind. Leaning delicately against the white railing, she twirled her parasol. Zane touched the pistol barrel to the brim of his cowboy hat in greeting.

"*Zane!*" Rose exclaimed as she set the rifle on the table.

"Quit dawdling. I want to practice my trick riding on Raven before Mama makes me do lessons." She stooped next to the leather supply trunk sitting open beside the gun table and carefully plucked several fist-sized balls from their box. They were made of green glass and were filled with flour so that when they broke, the audience would see a puff of white.

"Besides, those ladies are too high-society for you," she added for good measure.

Zane cocked one brow. "Louisville may be the most prosperous city in Kentucky," he said as he looked down the barrel of the revolver. "But ladies are the same in every town." He gave Rose a wink, then loaded the revolver with a single bullet. "Ready."

Rose tossed two glass balls high in the air. Kneeling on one knee, Zane aimed and quickly shot. When the balls shattered, the flour puffed in the air like smoke.

The lady with the parasol clapped, the sound muffled by her kid gloves.

"She's too highfalutin to get her hands dirty," Rose said. "Why would she look at you, a traveling cowboy?"

"'Cause I'm dashing and handsome?" Smiling, Zane tipped his hat to the lady. Lowering her parasol, she smiled coyly. Her auburn hair was swept into a chignon; a feathered hat was perched on top.

"Looks like a bird's nesting on her head," Rose giggled.

Zane laughed as he set the revolver on the table. "You're

the one to talk about fashion. Bare feet and bare limbs—you'll be the scandal of Louisville."

"One day I *will* be a scandal," Rose told him. "Excepting it'll be because I ride better than any man." She watched the lady sashay off to join the others, the bustle of her walking dress switching from side to side.

A loud whoop made Rose turn. A trio of cowboys mounted on ponies came charging through the gap in the fencing by the barns. As they galloped down the track, the ladies pressed against the inside railing and squealed.

"What in thunder? Those fools will run over the ladies." Zane set his revolver on the gun table. "Pack up my Colts for me," he said before setting off across the grass. "The ladies need an escort."

"And who's going to escort *you?*" Rose shouted, but Zane had already vaulted over the railing.

The three whooping riders slid their ponies to a halt in front of the ladies. When they raised their cowboy hats high, their ponies bowed on one knee. The ladies clapped.

Rose shook her head in disgust. *Bowing's for amateurs.* All spring, she and Raven had practiced the Dead Man's Drag and the Warrior Stand. Not one of the cowboys could outride her now. If only Mama would let her perform in the show. But Mama said no. And when Mama said no, there was no budging her.

She knew why Mama forbade it. Two years ago, Rose's papa had been killed when he fell from a horse during a performance, and Mama still grieved. *Maybe when you're grown up, you can ride in the show,* Mama said. Wasn't twelve almost grown?

Rose sighed as she wiped Zane's revolvers with a soft rag. Then she placed them in the red velvet–lined gun box. Zane's Colts were almost as special as he was, and she was proud that he trusted her with their care. Still, she was tired of being Zane's assistant. She was tired of running from the Sioux in "Raid on the Homesteaders' Cabin." She wanted her own act.

Rose closed the gun box and set it carefully on the grass. Then she folded up the gun table and laid it on top of the targets and trap launcher, already packed in the supply trunk. Later, the roustabouts would haul the trunk from the infield and store it in the supply tent until show time. Zane's Colts, however, were kept in the tent that Rose and Zane shared with their mother.

Picking up the gun box, Rose walked across the infield, the grass tickling her toes. A warm breeze lifted the brim of her cowboy hat, which shaded her face from the sun. When she reached the railing, she pushed the box through the slats. Hitching up her calf-length skirt and pinafore, she climbed over the fence and dropped onto the track, her bare feet making prints in the soft earth.

The show folks had set up camp on the west side of the track. Rose could see the canvas roofs of the mess tent and the supply tent and, beyond them, the rows of smaller, house-shaped tents where performers and crew lived. At the far end of the grounds, the Sioux, Cheyenne, and Pawnee had set up their tipis in separate camps. The tipis' tent poles jutted into the sky, and Rose could smell the smoke from the campfires that burned in front of every tipi.

"Rose!" Oliver Farley, Levi Frontier's thirteen-year-old son, waved at her from the arched entryway that led to the campground. "Your mama says it's time for lessons."

"Tell Mama you couldn't find me," Rose said as she crossed the track toward him.

Oliver gave her a blank look. "How can I tell your mama I didn't find you, Rose, when I *did* find you?"

"No, you didn't," Rose said firmly.

Oliver blinked behind his steel-rimmed glasses. He wore corduroy knickers, a white shirt, white stockings, and a yellow vest. There wasn't a speck of dirt on him any-where. *What a dandy,* Rose thought. But what did she expect? Oliver was only visiting his papa for the summer. Because Mr. Frontier traveled so much, Oliver usually lived with his rich grandmama in Boston.

"But that isn't *true*," Oliver protested, his voice cracking. He was gangly as a colt, a foot taller than Rose and skinny as a tent pole.

Rose sighed. "Oliver, haven't you ever told a lie?"

"Uh—" He thought hard, his Adam's apple bobbling in his neck.

"Okay, then, *don't* lie." Rose shoved Zane's gun box

into his arms. "Tell Mama you saw me, but you failed in your duty to bring me home because you were too lily-livered to take on a girl."

Oliver's face reddened. "I'm not too lily-livered," he said indignantly.

"And make sure you give her Zane's revolvers," Rose called as she headed down the track toward the barns. "Or my brother'll whip you!" she added as she took off running.

When she reached the rows of barns, she breathed in deeply. Manure, sweat, oats, leather, and—best of all—*horses*. She loved them all. Even the bangtails and broncs.

The stalls opened to the outside but were sheltered from the sun and rain by an overhanging roof. Rose strolled past the doors, greeting each horse with a pat. There was Mr. Frontier's high-stepping sorrel, Chief White Bear's spotted Appaloosa, and Zane's spirited paint stallion.

Finally, she reached Swift Raven's stall. The black pony stuck his head over the bottom door. Rose dug a sugar lump from the pocket of her pinafore and held it in the palm of her hand. Raven lipped it greedily, nuzzled her hand for more, then whinnied. From the other side of the barn came an answering whinny.

Rose plucked a currycomb from the wooden bucket by the door, ready to clean the pony. Not that Swift Raven was hers. She just pretended he was. Two months ago, when Chief White Bear had joined the Wild West show, he'd brought the pitch-black pony all the way from South Dakota. The first time Rose had ridden Raven bareback, she'd admired his short back, smooth gaits, and solid neck. *The perfect trick-riding pony.* Since then, White Bear had let Rose use Raven for practice, and she'd quickly fallen in love with the pony.

Unlatching the door, Rose slipped into the stall. She smoothed Raven's forelock, then laid her cheek on his warm neck. *If only he were hers.*

She was currying a patch of mud from Raven's side when she heard a voice declare, "Your mama says to come this minute or you *won't* be in the show tonight."

Rose stopped currying. She knew when she was beat. "Thanks for tattling on me, Oliver." Turning, she shot him her deadliest look. He was standing an arm's length from Raven's door.

Oliver's smirk faded. "I—I didn't tell her where you were, Rose. Honest. She just knew."

"I know you didn't." Rose opened the stall door. "Mama knows everything—I swear, she's part Gypsy." Dropping the currycomb in the bucket, she kissed Raven good-bye, then latched the door behind her. "Guess I can't avoid lessons forever."

As she headed toward the campground, Oliver fell into step beside her. "I like learning," he commented.

Rose snorted. *What a surprise.*

They walked in silence past the corrals of steers, mules,

and buffalo. Ahead of them, the campground bustled
with noise and activity. Cooks clanged iron pots. Someone
played a harmonica. Roustabouts hammered tent poles,
and a group of cowboys and Mexican *vaqueros* practiced
rope tricks. Rose's family had been traveling with the show
for several years, and now Rose couldn't imagine living
anywhere else.

"Your mama's got a surprise for you," Oliver finally said.

"What? A swat on my backside?"

Oliver's cheeks flamed at the mention of the unmen-
tionable. Rose hid her smile in the shadow of her hat brim.
Tormenting Oliver was so pleasurable.

"No, it's something to make lessons easier," Oliver
explained. "Grandmama sent it by train."

For a second, Rose wondered what it could be. But
then they walked through the Sioux camp, and she
breathed in the smoky smell of the campfires that several
women tended. The Sioux tipis were arranged in a circle,
their oval doors opening into the center. The buffalo-hide
coverings on the tents were painted with unique designs.
This afternoon, the smoke flaps at the tops of the tipis
were open to catch the fresh air.

Oliver's pa, Levi Frontier, came into the circle of tipis,
leading a tour group of gentlemen. The men were formally
dressed in dark morning coats, trousers, and bowler hats.
In contrast, Mr. Frontier wore fringed buckskin and a gray
Stetson hat. As he spoke, he stroked his flowing blond

mustache. Rose thought he was the most dashing man in the world—except for Zane, of course. Her brother's blue eyes and black hair captivated all the ladies.

"Gentlemen," Mr. Frontier said as he strolled in front of the group, "the Wild West is not a circus. There are no sideshows, freaks, or games of chance. What we bring you is an authentic picture of life beyond the Missouri."

He stopped in front of the largest tipi, home of Chief White Bear, Rose's friend. White Bear stepped through the opening. He wore a blue calico shirt and buckskin leggings decorated with beadwork. Rose waved to him, but his unblinking gaze was aimed over the heads of the visitors.

"Authentic," Mr. Frontier repeated with a flourish of his hand. "Gentlemen, I'd like to introduce you to the fearless and famous Chief of the Dakota Sioux."

Several of the gentlemen murmured and nodded. One man strode forward, hand outstretched. He had bushy red brows, a crooked nose, and a bristly red mustache. His bulbous stomach strained the buttons of his coat. "Chief White Bear," he stated, "it is an honor to finally meet you."

White Bear's eyes hardened. Tipping up his chin, he refused to answer the man or take his hand.

Rose wondered what was going on. Since White Bear had joined the show, he'd been reserved around white people, but he'd never been rude. He'd even profited from their curiosity, selling photographs of himself for fifty cents apiece.

The man sputtered indignantly. "Frontier, tell this Indian to show me some respect."

Mr. Frontier put his arm around the man's shoulder and steered him away from the tipi. "Another day, perhaps. I believe a visit with Billy Dees, our broncobuster, is in order," he said, deftly leading the group away.

Rose stared after the departing men, then looked back at White Bear, who hadn't moved. Beside her, Oliver shifted uneasily. "I'll meet you at your tent," he whispered before darting after the departing group.

Slowly, Rose walked up to the chief. She stood beside him, waiting for his acknowledgment so she could speak. Nearby, the Sioux women silently resumed their activities.

"Humph," he finally said. "How fast that red-haired man forgets."

"Forgets what, Ma-to-sea?" Rose asked, using his Sioux name. "Who is he?"

"General Judson." White Bear spat out the name. "Fought against my people at the Powder River."

"That was almost ten years ago," Rose said. White Bear and his sons had told her about the battle.

White Bear narrowed his eyes. "The years don't matter. The Sioux will never forget. As long as the sun rises and sets, that man will be our enemy."

Rose didn't reply, but the hatred in her friend's voice made her shudder.

LET THE WILD WEST BEGIN!

"Rose Hannah Taylor! *What* is all
over your pinafore?" Mama scolded
the minute Rose stepped into their
tent. Mama was seated at her treadle
sewing machine, which was set up by
the door to catch the light.

"Horsehair, slobber, grass." Rose
hung her hat on the clothes tree behind
the sewing machine. "If I had a leather riding outfit like
Billy Dees, I wouldn't dirty my pinafore."

Mama pursed her lips. "Last time I looked, you were
a young lady, Rose Hannah. Not a cowboy like Billy Dees."
Rising from the sewing machine, she turned Rose around
and untied her pinafore.

"That's not my fault," Rose grumbled.

Putting her hands on Rose's shoulders, Mama spun her
around. Rose had grown so tall, they were almost eye to
eye. "That's enough sass. It's bad enough I allow you to run
wild all over camp like a mustang. A proper daughter would

be cooking and sewing. Now hurry and get cleaned up. Oliver's waiting for us in the headquarters tent. And bring your schoolbooks," she added as she pulled her bonnet from the clothes tree. "I couldn't find them anywhere."

"Yes, ma'am." Rose took off her pinafore and walked to the back of the tent, her bare feet thumping on the tent's wood-plank floor. The left side of the tent was curtained off with a faded quilt hanging from a tent pole. Rose ducked around the quilt and stepped into the makeshift bedroom she and her mama shared. Since they moved from town to town, their furnishings and belongings were sparse. The room had two sleeping cots, a trunk, and a porcelain washbasin and pitcher on a small wooden stand. Another quilt hung down the center of the tent, partitioning off a small area on the right for Zane.

Rose tossed her dirty pinafore on her cot. Then she knelt in front of the trunk and pulled out a clean, folded pinafore. Digging deeper, she found her geography and spelling books under her drawers and stockings.

Lessons. She'd almost rather be cooking and sewing.

Rose tied on her pinafore and picked up her books. Before leaving, she stopped by her mama's sewing machine. On the sewing chair was a piece of cream-colored suede. She touched the leather, glorying in its softness. Her mama sewed and mended all the performers' costumes. This piece of leather was so fine, Rose knew it would one day be a fancy jacket for Mr. Frontier or Zane.

As Rose ran from the dim tent, her footsteps sounded like drumbeats on the wooden walkways that connected the tents. When she stopped in front of the headquarters tent, she heard a clacking noise. The tent flaps were tied back, and she could see Oliver hunched over William Pearson's rolltop desk. Mr. Pearson stood beside him, thumbs hooked in the lapels of his elegant long suit coat. He had fuzzy muttonchop sideburns, heavy jowls, and a thick chest. He was co-owner and manager of the show, in charge of publicity, travel arrangements, bookings, and finances—everything that Mr. Frontier hated to do. He also had a booming voice and announced the acts during each show.

"A fine instrument," Mr. Pearson was saying when Rose came into the tent. "Should certainly make correspondence easier."

"Rose, come look at what Oliver's grandmother sent him," Mama said. "It's a typewriter."

"What's a typewriter?" Rose asked.

"It's a writing machine. Come see!" Oliver said as his fingers pounded at a keyboard. Rose watched in amazement as long metal arms lifted up and stamped letters on a white piece of paper. "You try it," he said. He stood and pushed Rose down into the canvas chair. "I'm writing a thank-you letter to Grandmama."

Leaning closer, Rose read the letter that Oliver had started.

May 20, 1886

Dear Grandmama,

The Remington typewriter came today. Mr. Pearson,
Mrs. Taylor, Rose, and I thank you. Mr. Pearson will
use it for business. Rose and I will use it for lessons and
writing letters.

Rose sat back in the chair and raised her hands to the
keys. "What do you want me to type?"

"Tell her about Chief White Bear," Oliver suggested.

"Okay." Hesitantly, Rose tapped a key with one finger.
When the arm hit the paper, nothing happened.

"Harder," Oliver said impatiently.

Rose hit the key again. This time the arm flew up and
a *c* appeared on the paper. Behind her, Mama clapped.
Grinning, Rose tapped an *h*, then paused, her pointer finger
hovering in the air. "How do you spell 'chief'?"

Oliver rolled his eyes. "Here, let me do it." He bumped
her off the chair. "It'll be sundown before you get his
name written."

Mr. Pearson chuckled. "Oliver, I do believe I'll make
you my secretary." He waved his hand at the piles of papers
tucked in the cubbyholes of his heavy oak desk. Every time
the show moved to another town, it took five men to lift
the desk onto a wagon, then transfer it to the train. But
Mr. Pearson refused to leave it behind. "There's enough
correspondence here to keep us busy your entire visit."

"That's fine with me, sir!" Oliver declared.

Mr. Pearson pulled out his gold pocket watch. "I'm due for an appointment," he told them. "Carry on with your studies."

When he left, Mama handed Rose a slate and a piece of chalk. "While Oliver's typing his letter, you may work on your multiplication tables. Start with the fours and—"

"But Mama," Rose interrupted, "why do I need to learn to multiply? A horse only has one set of four legs."

"What about when you own six head of horses?" Mama said patiently. "And they all need four shoes?"

"Oh." Rose pondered the problem as she plopped down in Mr. Pearson's rocker. She started to tuck her bare legs under her skirt, but Mama frowned disapprovingly. With a sigh, she crossed them at the ankles and began to write:

$$2 \times 4 = 8 \qquad 3 \times 4 = 13 \qquad 4 \times 4 = 16$$

"I can't wait to show Mr. Frontier my new typewriter," Oliver said, pulling the finished letter from the carriage.

Mr. Frontier. Rose wondered why Oliver addressed his father so formally. Although her own father was dead, she would always think of him as *Papa.*

"Rose, three times four is not thirteen," Mama admonished. "A lady needs to learn arithmetic even if she's going to be a star in a Wild West show."

Rose glanced up and noticed the gleam in Mama's eyes. She dropped the slate on her lap. "What do you mean?"

"Mr. Frontier has a new role for you in the show tonight."

"You mean I get to be more than just a settler?" All spring, Rose had played the settlers' daughter who was captured by Sioux warriors in "Raid on the Homesteaders' Cabin." "And more than Zane's assistant?"

"You'll still do that. But starting tonight, Mr. Frontier wants you to ride in the Dry Gulch Stage during the grand parade."

Rose's heart started to beat faster. The grand parade was the opening act for the whole show. All the performers rode around the track, serenaded by the Cowboy Band and cheered wildly by the audience.

"And do I get to ride on the stage during the shoot-out with the bandits?" Rose interrupted excitedly.

"Yes." Mama smiled, and for a minute, the tired lines around her eyes softened. When the Wild West show first started, Mama had played the beautiful belle on the Dry Gulch Stage. When the bandits attacked, she helped fend them off with a derringer hidden in her bodice. The audience had loved it. But after Rose's father died, Mama never performed in another show. She'd packed away her costumes of velvet and lace. The joy had gone out of acting, she'd told Rose. Now, instead of performing in front of thousands, she worked alone, hunched over the sewing machine until her shoulders ached and her vision blurred.

Rose jumped from the rocker. "Do I get to fire a derringer?"

Mama laughed. "Perhaps after you and Zane practice

for a spell. We don't want anyone's foot shot off. This evening, you'll be the official guide and escort for the dignitaries that Mr. Frontier's invited to ride in the stagecoach. That means perfect manners, young lady."

"Oh yes, Mama, and thank you." Rose gave her a hug.

A heavy sigh made them both glance over at Oliver. He was still sitting in front of the typewriter, staring down at the letter in his hand. "I wish I could be part of the show," he mumbled as if talking to the letter.

Rose bit her lip. Since Oliver's arrival a week ago, his father had paid him scant attention. "Mama, why don't we ask Mr. Frontier if Oliver can be in the stagecoach, too?" she asked. "He's so skinny, he'll take up only a hair of room."

Oliver looked up. Behind his glasses, his eyes grew as round as cookpots. "You think Mr. Frontier would allow it?"

Mama ruffled Oliver's hair. "I think he will. Now back to lessons, you two," she said firmly.

"Yes, ma'am!" Rose grabbed up her slate. Squinting down at the numbers, she tried to concentrate as she wrote:

$$4 \times 3 = 12 \quad 4 \times 4 = 16 \quad 4 \times 5 = 21$$

But all Rose could think about was tonight's show. Riding in the Dry Gulch Stage wasn't the same as having her own act. And it wasn't near as exciting as performing tricks on her pony. But it was a start.

"Oh, Rose, you look beautiful!" Mama gasped two hours later. It was early evening, almost show time. Rose and Oliver had finished lessons and eaten an early dinner with the other performers. Now Rose was dressing for the show.

Rose wrinkled her nose. "I feel like a stuffed goose." She was wearing one of Mama's old costumes. Mama had hurriedly altered it, but it was still too big. The layers of petticoats plus the floor-length velvet skirt over its hoop-shaped crinoline weighed as much as a hay bale. "How am I supposed to fight off robbers all gussied up like this?"

"Leave the fighting to the cavalry," Mama said, laughing. Opening a small jar, she started to smooth rouge on Rose's cheeks.

Rose jerked away. "No rouge, Mama. And no lacy parasol either—unless I can use it to hit a bandit over the head. I refuse to look like a preening ostrich."

Mama sighed. "You mean you refuse to look like a lady," she said softly. She held out a pair of high-heeled, lace-up boots. "How about these?"

Rose groaned and shook her head. "No one will know I'm barefoot under all this froth!" Gathering up the heavy skirts, she gave her mother a peck on the cheek and hurried from the tent.

"Rose? Is that *you?*" Oliver exclaimed when she met him outside. Oliver was dressed as usual, but behind him, Rose could see other costume-clad performers heading to the arched entrance that led to the track.

"You don't have to sound so addled," Rose said. Chin high, she tried to keep up with him as they made their way to the show grounds, but her feet kept getting tangled in her skirts. "Oh, bloody blazes!" she finally blurted.

"Rose!" Oliver gasped.

"Oh, shush, Oliver. If you were wearing this getup, you'd cuss, too."

When they reached the entrance to the racetrack, they made their way through the milling crowd of performers. Everyone was preparing for the grand parade. The Cowboy Band musicians tuned up their instruments. A half-dozen *vaqueros* in sombreros and fancy bolero jackets rode around a herd of longhorns, keeping them settled. The uniformed cavalry officers checked their horses' saddles and bridles.

Standing on tiptoe, Rose peered across the track to the grandstand. It looked filled, yet she could see a line of people still waiting to buy tickets. Tonight would be Mr. Frontier's favorite kind of show—sold out!

Near the entrance to the track, Rose spotted Zane loading his supply trunk onto a cart hitched to Mr. Big Ears, the donkey. Zane looked handsome in his black, wide-brimmed hat, black pants tucked into gleaming black boots, white leather vest over a black shirt, and leather gun belt slung low on his hips. Rose headed over to join him.

"May I help you, lovely miss?" Zane asked when she came up.

Rose's jaw dropped. "Zane, it's me!"

He grinned. "I know it's you. Your dirty toes are peeking out from under your petticoats," he teased, adding, "Are you too fancy to be my assistant tonight, Miss Taylor? Will I have to invite a young lady from the audience to hold my target?"

"One glance at the dashing Sharpshootin' Cowboy, and the young ladies will be too faint to hold your target," Rose teased right back.

"Rose, we're ready to board!" Oliver called. He was motioning toward the stagecoach, which was parked by the track entrance. Pop Whittaker, the coach's driver, was checking the harnesses of the six-horse team. Billy Dees, a shotgun resting in the crook of his arm, sat in the driver's seat, holding the reins for Pop.

Picking up her skirts, Rose hurried over to the stage-coach. Oliver stood with several grownups in front of the coach door. *The dignitaries,* Rose guessed. She recognized General Judson's red whiskers and indignant voice. He was arguing with a tall, slender man wearing a top hat and double-breasted gray coat with satin lapels. A third man in a top hat hovered nearby. Holding his arm was a woman stylishly dressed in a silk, ankle-length overcoat.

Mr. Frontier bustled up. He wore his show costume of white buckskin. "Gentlemen, Mayor and Mrs. Reed." He nodded his head to the couple. "This is no time to argue politics. The grand parade will be starting any minute. You need to board the stagecoach."

"Fine. However, don't sit me next to Senator North here." Judson poked a silver-handled cane at the tall man. "The only reason I'm traveling in the same conveyance with North is because we are both your guests, Levi."

Senator North touched his finger to his top hat. "I aim to be civil to a war hawk, General. I hope you can be respectful of my views."

Judson sputtered. Rose had no idea what "war hawk" meant, but obviously the general didn't like it.

"Better a hawk than a bleeding dove who wants to coddle the Indians as if they were children," Judson growled.

Coddle the Indians? Rose snorted. Letting the Sioux keep what land the white man hadn't taken hardly sounded like coddling to her. No wonder Chief White Bear wouldn't shake the general's hand.

"Gentlemen!" Mr. Frontier's tone was firm. When the two men hushed, Mr. Frontier offered his arm to Mayor Reed's wife. "Ma'am, step carefully on this block of wood, then onto the metal step." With a rustle of silk, the mayor's wife climbed into the coach, her skirts filling the doorway before she pulled them in after her.

"Rose?" Mr. Frontier offered her his arm.

She ignored it. "Just 'cause I'm dressed like a lady doesn't mean I'm crippled," she muttered. As Rose stepped onto the block, her foot caught the edge of her skirt. She pitched headfirst into the stagecoach, her petticoats swelling around her in a wave of fabric.

Behind her, Oliver guffawed.

If I ever get untangled, Rose vowed from beneath the yards of velvet, *I'll throttle his scrawny neck.*

"Take my hand, dear," the mayor's wife said from her seat in the coach. With Mrs. Reed's help, Rose finally hoisted herself into the coach and sat down across from the mayor's wife on the leather-upholstered seat that ran along the back. Oliver scrambled in after her and sat next to Mrs. Reed. He was opposite Rose and so close that their knees almost touched. Mayor Reed sat down beside Oliver, who immediately began telling him and his wife all about the new typewriter.

Pulling himself through the coach door, General Judson plumped down at Rose's left while Senator North climbed in through the facing door and sat on her right.

"So, North," Judson said, "I take it you'll be voting against the Dawes Allotment Act."

"You can count on it," North replied. "And I'll vote against any other bill that aims to steal the Indians' land."

"The Indians' land?" Judson snorted. "Ha. They have no rights to the land. They have no deeds, no legal documents recognized in a court of law."

North twisted in his seat to face the general and shook his finger in front of Rose's face. "You mean to say the fact that they have lived on the land for countless generations has no bearing on the matter?"

"Oh, sirs, listen!" Rose piped up, hoping to distract

them. "Mr. Pearson is introducing the grand parade!"

The two men closed their mouths and sat back in their seats. Silently, they stared straight ahead, their expressions grim. Rose squirmed, feeling like a strand of barbed wire between them.

Then the Cowboy Band began playing "My Old Kentucky Home," and Rose forgot about the men and their argument. The crowd in the grandstand began to cheer, and a shiver of excitement raced through her as Mr. Pearson's booming voice announced, "Let the Wild West begin!"

CHAPTER 3

ATTACK ON THE DRY GULCH STAGE

Pop Whittaker poked his head through the stagecoach window. "Y'all ready to join the grand parade?"

"Yes, s-s-sir!" Oliver stuttered. Rose nodded excitedly. Mrs. Reed twittered nervously. Judson pulled out his pocket watch. "'Bout time," he grumbled.

"Gentlemen, spit yer tobaccy on the leeward side," Pop warned. "Everybody sit tight if the team runs off. And hang on if the coach tips over."

Mrs. Reed blanched, but Rose grinned. Every show, Pop gave the same advice, even though the team had never once run off, and the coach had never tipped over.

The stagecoach creaked as Pop climbed back into the driver's seat. Then Rose heard the crack of the whip and Pop yelled, "Hiya!"

The coach lurched forward. Rose could hear the pounding of the horses' hooves as they trotted onto the track to the tune of "My Old Kentucky Home." The harness jingled. The stagecoach swayed. Oliver held his stomach, his face green.

As they rounded the bend and headed toward the grandstand, Rose leaned across Senator North and waved out the window. Up ahead, she could see Zane and Mr. Frontier, mounted on their showy stallions, leading the parade. Buckskin-clad Indians, mounted on ponies, came next. Behind the stagecoach rode the Mexican *vaqueros,* who used their whips and lassos to move the longhorn steers and buffalo along the track.

"It's a sold-out show," Mayor Reed said as he peered out the window too. "From newsboys to bankers, the whole city of Louisville is attending."

Rose believed it. As they passed the grandstand, she waved to Mr. Pearson perched high on the roofed platform of the steward's tower, where he announced the acts through a megaphone. The roar from the audience was deafening. People filled the tiered grandstand from top to bottom and crowded along the rails. It was, indeed, a sold-out show.

The grand procession paraded twice around the track. By the time the stagecoach rumbled out through the arched entryway, even Oliver was waving at the crowd.

As soon as Pop halted the coach outside the gate, Rose clambered past Senator North, saying, "Excuse me, excuse me." She jumped down, careful to lift her skirts, and ran to assist Zane. The Sharpshootin' Cowboy was the first act.

She spotted Zane, still mounted on Comanche on the other side of the cavalry. He was waiting for the parade of animals and people to exit the track so he could make his grand entrance. That was Rose's cue to drive Mr. Big Ears and the supply trunk onto the infield and set up for the act.

"And here he is, folks," she heard Mr. Pearson announce from the steward's tower. "The dashing, the daring, the most accurate shot in the west—*and* the east—Zane Taylor, Sharpshootin' Cowboy!"

Zane and Comanche galloped through the gate and onto the track. They raced around the bend, a flash of black and white. On the straightaway in front of the grandstand, Zane slid Comanche to a halt. The stallion reared, his hooves pawing the air. Zane waved his hat, the Cowboy Band played "Dixie Land," and the audience went wild.

Gathering her petticoats and skirt, Rose climbed onto the tiny cart seat. "Okay, Big Ears, that's our cue," she whispered. She slapped the reins on the donkey's back and he ambled onto the track, pulling the cart with the trunk. Mr. Big Ears was notoriously stubborn, but Rose bribed him with sugar cubes to get him on and off the show grounds without a fight.

The donkey trotted across the dirt track and through the gap in the fence to the grassy infield. In front of the grandstand, Zane thrilled the audience with his lariat tricks. Rose fed Mr. Big Ears his sugar cube, then quickly took the gun table from the cart, unfolded it, and set it up on the grass. Next she pulled the clay pigeons and the trap launcher from the open trunk and set them up next to the table. She was used to wearing a simple calico dress, her settlers' daughter costume. Tonight, every time she turned, her voluminous skirts knocked something over.

"Like wearing a tent," Rose grumbled. She glanced at the audience, hoping no one noticed her clumsiness. They were too busy watching Zane lasso a gentleman sitting in the front row. The man bellowed like a steer and the crowd laughed. Zane released the lariat and, with a "Yee-ha!," spurred Comanche into a gallop.

As they came racing around the track, Rose quickly counted out ten glass balls. Comanche cantered into the infield. When he was exactly four strides from her, Rose threw the balls into the air. Pulling a gun from his holster, Zane shattered them all before they fell to the ground.

Comanche slowed and Zane leaped off smoothly. He looped the reins over the saddle horn, and the stallion trotted from the track, where Billy Dees caught him. For the next twenty minutes, Zane performed shooting tricks. He shot clay pigeons while standing on his head. He shot lighted candles off a stool while lying on his back. He looked into a mirror and shot glass balls that Rose threw into the air behind him. Rose tossed up a handful of coins and with a single blast of a shotgun he hit them in midair.

For the grand finale, Rose took a pack of playing cards from the trunk. She held up two aces and showed them to the crowd. Spurs jingling, Zane strode to the gun table. Carefully, he lifted each of his Colts from their box and inspected them with exaggerated care.

A drum rolled, and Mr. Pearson announced, "Ladies and gentlemen, the Sharpshootin' Cowboy will attempt to shoot two aces while his assistant holds the cards in her bare hands! This trick has never—I repeat, *never*—been attempted before. Please, let's have silence, so the champion can concentrate."

As the drumroll continued, Rose and Zane positioned themselves about twenty feet apart. Rose faced Zane and held the cards aloft. Zane aimed both revolvers, then suddenly lowered his arms and shook his head as if he were losing faith. Murmurs rose in the crowd.

Rose tried not to grin. Zane was such an actor. He'd practiced the trick a hundred times, and he performed it perfectly every show.

Without warning, he spun and shot. *Crack! Crack!* The sharp retort made Rose's ears ring. She held the two cards out to the audience, showing the holes shot neatly through the middle of each ace.

The audience clapped and cheered. Comanche trotted into the infield, the reins looped over the saddle horn. Zane vaulted into the saddle and cantered the stallion toward the railing. The crowd gasped as Comanche jumped over the railing onto the track, then whirled on his hind legs in front of the grandstand. Handkerchiefs and flowers rained onto Zane's head. Rose saw him catch a handkerchief and press it to his cheek. Glancing up into the stands, she saw the smiling face of the auburn-haired lady.

"I'm half-deaf, and he gets all the glory," Rose muttered as she repacked the Colts in their gun box, collapsed the gun table, and packed up the supply trunk. Zane galloped from the track just as the four Pony Express riders cantered in and positioned themselves for their exhibition.

Rose had five minutes to get out of their way. She slammed the trunk lid down and climbed onto the seat of the cart. "Git up, Mr. Big Ears." The donkey broke into a speedy trot. Rose tipped backward and her bare feet flew into the air. The crowd roared with laughter.

Furious, Rose whapped at her billowing skirts. Mr. Big Ears trotted from the track. Billy Dees was standing by the entrance waiting for his broncobusting act. He caught the donkey's harness. "Why, Miss Rose, I do believe you forgot your dancing shoes," he said, his leathery face breaking into such a huge grin that Rose couldn't help but laugh, too.

"I reckon I did, Billy Dees."

Zane sauntered over, the lace handkerchief peeking from his vest. "Good show tonight, Rose."

Rose plucked out the handkerchief. "A souvenir?" Placing it under her nose, she sniffed loudly. "Lily of the valley, perhaps?"

With a frown, Zane snatched it from her and tucked it back in his vest. "None of your business."

"Whoo-eee," Billy Dees hooted. "I do believe the sharp-shootin' champ has been roped and hog-tied."

"Rose, make sure my gun box gets back to the tent," Zane said. "I have to meet a lady." Turning smartly, he strode off.

Rose stared after him. Was he going to meet the auburn-haired lady? Zane had admirers in every town, but she'd never seen him serious about one of them.

A wrangler unhitched Mr. Big Ears, and two roustabouts came to carry the trunk to the supply tent. Before they hauled it off, Rose retrieved Zane's gun box. He'd tan her hide if anyone else handled his Colts.

"Rose? Ready to board the stage? 'Attack on the Dry Gulch Stage' is next," Mr. Frontier called as he strode up, Oliver dogging his boot heels. Oliver's face was still green.

"Yes, sir. I just need to run these back to the tent," Rose said.

Mr. Frontier nodded. "Hurry, then. I need you to sit between the senator and the general again and keep them from fisticuffs. When the bandits stop the stage, remind all the passengers to act afraid."

"Yes, sir." Rose raced off, her bare feet pummeling the dirt. She'd show Levi Frontier she could handle this respon-sibility. Perhaps then he'd begin to realize that she could handle her own act.

The campground was deserted, and the setting sun cast deepening shadows along the wooden walkways. Rose ran up to their tent, threw back the flaps, and hollered, "Mama! I'm leaving Zane's gun box on your sewing table." Then she spun and headed back to the track, weaving through the mounted cavalry soldiers who would ride to the passengers' rescue.

Pop Whittaker was ready to shut the stagecoach door. Since Billy Dees was busting broncs in the infield, Mustang Jack took his place, riding shotgun next to Pop. A trunk of "gold" sat behind him on top of the coach.

"You're just in time, Miss Rose," Pop said. "Billy Dees is about to git throwed off Old Lightning. That's our cue to enter." Holding her elbow, he helped her inside the coach. Her skirts filled the narrow aisle. Batting and tugging at the fabric, Rose maneuvered between the general and the senator, who were turned away from each other.

"Britches sure would be handier," she said. When she finally corralled her petticoats and sat down, she noticed that Oliver wasn't between the mayor and his wife.

"He had a touch of dyspepsia," Mrs. Reed said. "I recommended Dr. Benjamin's Tonic."

Rose grimaced. Even when it was laced with molasses, the remedy was worse than the ailment.

"Here comes Billy Dees," Pop Whittaker announced from the driver's seat. "He's limping but he's grinning. He must've whupped Old Lightning." Pop thumped on the side of the coach. "Time for the Dry Gulch Stage, folks. Hang on tight! Yee-ha!"

The whip cracked, and the team of horses broke into a trot. Rose grabbed Senator North's arm to keep from tipping. The coach rattled and bumped as the horses cantered onto the track.

Minutes later, gunshots rang out. "I do believe we're being attacked!" Mayor Reed exclaimed dramatically. His wife clutched his arm. Her veiled hat had slipped onto her forehead, and she was smiling nervously.

"It's a gang of bandits," Rose hollered over the shooting. The performers shot harmless blanks, but the noise was still deafening.

"They must be after the trunk of gold!" the senator said, getting into the act.

General Judson harrumphed.

"Hiya!" Rose heard Pop Whittaker yell to the team. On top of the coach, Mustang Jack returned fire with his shotgun. The horses galloped around the homestretch bend toward the grandstand. The plan was for the bandits to halt the coach in front of the crowd.

With a cry, Mrs. Reed pointed out her window. A bandit had steered his horse beside the coach. A red handkerchief covered his nose and mouth. "Stop the stage or I'll shoot!" the man ordered.

Since Rose had seen the act a hundred times, she knew the bandit was Con Hardy riding his plucky cow pony, Belle.

Con had once been the real-life sheriff of Durango, Colorado. Before White Bear had let her use Swift Raven, Rose had often practiced her tricks on Belle. Tonight, however, Con and Belle were outlaws.

"By golly, this does feel like the Old West," Senator North said, grinning like a kid. Then gunshots rang so loud and fast that Rose plugged her ears.

As the coach began to slow, General Judson let out a groan and fell hard against Rose's shoulder. Rose grinned, amazed that the general was finally getting into the act.

"It's all right, sir," Rose reassured him. "Any minute the cavalry will be along to save us."

But Judson slumped further, his head dropping into Rose's lap. Startled, Rose shrank away from him. What in thunderation was the general doing?

"Um, sir?" Rose lightly shook both his shoulders. "You can quit acting now." Judson didn't stir. Something warm dripped onto Rose's right hand. She held it up. In the dim light, she could see dark splotches on her fingers. She peered around the top of the general's head. Something red trickled down his right temple and plopped onto her skirt. It was blood!

Rose gasped. "Senator North! Tell Pop Whittaker to halt the stage. General Judson's hurt!"

CHAPTER 4
SUSPICION

S enator North glanced at Rose.
"Nothing could hurt General Judson.
He's too hardheaded."

"Sir, please." Rose showed him her
bloody fingers and pointed at Judson,
still slumped in her lap. "There's blood
on the right side of his head."

The senator's eyes widened under
his top hat. Twisting in his seat, he bent over to check the
side of Judson's head. "By gosh, it looks like a bullet wound!"

Jumping up, North reached out the window and banged
on the side of the coach. "Whittaker! Stop at once! The
general's hurt!"

As part of the act, the coach had already slowed in front
of the grandstand so the bandits could rob the passengers.
"Whoa!" Pop Whittaker hollered, and the coach rattled to
a stop. A masked man threw open the door.

"Everybody out," he growled fiercely. "No dawdling
or we'll shoot you all."

"Sir, we have an injured man on board," Senator North protested, but the masked man grabbed his arm and started to pull him from the coach.

Rose realized that Con probably thought Senator North was playing along with the show.

"Mr. Hardy," Rose said firmly. Leaning forward, she put her hand on his wrist and looked him straight in the eyes. "This passenger is truly hurt and needs help. We need to get the coach off the track right away without alarming the audience."

Con's brows rose in surprise; then he nodded once. "Will do, Miss Rose." Shutting the door, he hollered, "Mount up, men! This stagecoach has so much loot, we'll take it to our hideout!"

"Con!" another bandit yelled. "The cavalry's coming!"

"Don't matter, Joe. We're gittin' out of here!" Con hollered back.

Rose saw Con climb up onto the top of the coach. She didn't know what he said to Pop Whittaker, but the stage-coach jerked forward, and in a few minutes they were bumping swiftly around the track, the mounted bandits escorting them to the exit.

A bugle blew. Rose peered out the window and glimpsed the cavalry heading full tilt after them. Levi Frontier on his sorrel stallion, Ranger, was leading the charge. The cavalry caught up just as the stagecoach swerved out the arched entryway, tipping dangerously.

"What in tarnation!" she heard Mr. Frontier yell when the coach rattled to a halt outside the track. "What happened to the act? Con, was this your cockamamie idea?"

Senator North leaped from the coach. "Sir, I take full responsibility. General Judson's hurt. Looks like he was shot during the act."

"Shot?" Mr. Frontier repeated, and Rose could hear the disbelief in his voice. She looked down at Judson, his head still cradled in her lap. He lay motionless, his eyes closed and his skin pallid. Blood had oozed from his wound onto her skirt, staining it dark brown.

"How can he be shot?" Mr. Frontier looked into the stagecoach, and Rose's eyes filled with tears.

"I don't know, but he's surely hurt, sir," she whispered.

"Let's get him out of there," Mr. Frontier commanded, and several cavalrymen reached inside and lifted the general from the coach. As Mayor Reed followed after them, Rose heard Mr. Frontier order the Cowboy Band to entertain the audience until the next act.

Mrs. Reed held out a handkerchief to Rose. She looked shaken, but she put a steadying hand on Rose's shoulder. "You were very brave, dear. Braver than my daughter Abigail would have been under such trying circumstances."

"Do you think the general's going to die?" Rose asked, her voice quivering.

Mrs. Reed shook her head. "I don't know. Let's hope he'll be all right." Then her husband reached into the coach, and she took his hand to climb out.

Rose couldn't move; she was too numb. She couldn't understand what had happened. Senator North said it looked as if the general had been shot. But the bandits always used blank cartridges. When the guns were fired, the powder made noise, but no bullet came out of the cartridge. What had gone wrong?

Turning in the seat, she stared at the back wall of the coach. If someone had shot a real bullet, there would likely be a hole. She poked around until she felt splintered wood. Then her fingertips touched something smooth and hard. She peered closer. A bullet was stuck tight in the wood.

Rose's stomach twisted. Someone *had* used a real bullet. Who would want to shoot General Judson?

White Bear's angry voice filled her head. *As long as the sun rises and sets, that man will be our enemy.*

White Bear? Rose shivered as she turned back around. She couldn't stand to think that her friend had anything to do with the shooting. Except White Bear obviously hated the general, and Rose knew that he and the other Sioux in the show were excellent shots. Had one of them hidden in the shadows and shot the general when the coach swept past?

"Rose? Are you coming?" Mrs. Reed peered into the stagecoach.

"Yes, ma'am." Rose climbed out, her heart as heavy as her skirts. In the distance, she heard Mr. Pearson announce to the crowd, "And now, the famous Cowboy Band will play 'Oh! Susanna.'"

As the first notes of the song floated over the track, a horse-drawn ambulance pulled up behind the stagecoach. Mr. Frontier had one on hand for every show. It wasn't unusual for a cowboy to take a tumble off his horse or for a steer to run over a *vaquero*.

The cavalrymen placed General Judson on a litter, and an attendant pressed a cloth to the wound on his head. Rose stood by the stagecoach and watched as the attendants hoisted the general into the back of the ambulance. In front of her, Mr. Frontier was talking with the mayor. Mustang Jack and Pop Whittaker were checking the bandits' guns.

Looking for real bullets, Rose knew. Would they find any? Had one of Con Hardy's bandits loaded a real bullet by mistake?

In the arena, the Cowboy Band began the rousing refrain of "Oh! Susanna," and the audience sang and clapped to the music. Rose watched as Pop Whittaker hurried up to Mr. Frontier and spoke to him in a low voice.

As the ambulance rumbled off, Mayor Reed said, "Frontier, I am deeply concerned about the safety of the citizenry. I know the show is billed as authentic; however, I didn't expect someone to get shot."

"Sir, my men have inspected the weapon of every bandit who was performing when the general was hurt,"

Mr. Frontier said. "Pop Whittaker assured me that all were loaded with blank cartridges. General Judson couldn't have been shot."

Just then, a portly man marched up to the mayor. He was flanked by two patrolmen in uniform. "Perhaps Chief Whallen of the Louisville Police can determine what happened," Mayor Reed said, referring to the man. "I expect you will give him your utmost cooperation, Frontier."

Chief Whallen shook hands with Mr. Frontier, then said, "I'm going to inspect the coach. Then I'll need to ask you several questions about the shooting, sir."

The chief and his men stepped toward the coach. Mayor Reed turned to Mr. Frontier and said stiffly, "I must escort my wife home now. She's seen quite enough for one evening. Good night, Frontier."

As the mayor strode off with his wife on his arm, Mr. Frontier lifted his Stetson. Rose came up beside him. "Sir," she whispered, "I don't know how it got there, but a bullet is lodged in the back of the stagecoach."

Mr. Frontier looked sharply at her, then over at the stagecoach. The two patrolmen had climbed inside while Chief Whallen stood by the door, giving orders.

"Well, one thing we know for sure," Mr. Frontier said. "Whoever shot the man was a dang good marksman. Maybe I should sign him up for the show." He snorted at his joke, then sighed wearily. "I just hope Mayor Reed doesn't decide to close down the show."

"Oh gosh, sir, if he did, it would be all my fault," Rose blurted, her lower lip trembling. "You entrusted me with the general's care. I failed you."

"You did fine, Miss Rose." He patted her shoulder. Then, smoothing his long blond hair, he settled the Stetson back on his head. "Time for me to face the formidable Chief Whallen and his questions."

When Rose didn't move, he glanced down at her. "So what are you waiting for, miss—molasses to harden? Git out of that fancy gown and into your settler's bonnet and calico. We've got a show to put on!"

"Yes, sir." Picking up her skirts, Rose ran back to the campground, glad that Mr. Frontier wasn't angry with her. The sun had set, and lanterns lighted the walkways. Several performers stood in clusters talking, undoubtedly about the shooting, Rose figured. She was dying to tell Mama about it as well.

"Mama!" she called as she raced into the tent. A single lantern hung from the middle tent pole and cast a golden glow into the corners, but Mama wasn't there.

Plucking her calico dress from the clothes tree, Rose darted behind the quilt partition and began to wrestle with the hooks on the front of the velvet dress. Oh, where was Mama when she needed her!

Finally, she got the bodice unhooked, and the velvet dress dropped to the floor. She wiggled out of the layers of petticoats, feeling pounds lighter in only her cotton chemise and a single petticoat. Quickly, she pulled the calico dress over her head as she started toward the front of the tent.

Without slowing, she snatched her bonnet from the clothes tree and ran back to the track, tying the bonnet strings under her chin as she went. The Cowboy Band was riding around the track on horseback, finishing up a song. Rose stopped at the entrance to catch her breath.

In the infield, the roustabouts were setting up the props for "Raid on the Homesteaders' Cabin." They had carried out a small log cabin, pulled out a Conestoga wagon, laid a stack of firewood near the cabin door, and "planted" a tree—a sapling that had been cut just for the show.

"Rose." Oliver came up to the entrance, a rifle slung awkwardly over his shoulder. He was bareheaded and wore a homespun shirt and baggy pants held up with suspenders. "Mr. Frontier said I can be a settler, too."

"Oh?" Any other time, Rose would have been annoyed to share the spotlight. All year it had been just her and Annabel Whittaker, Pop's daughter, playing the home-steaders' family. But the shooting had her spooked, and she was honestly glad that Oliver would be performing, too.

"Did Mr. Frontier explain what you're supposed to do?" Rose asked.

Oliver fidgeted uneasily. "When the Sioux set the tree on fire, I'm to run out of the cabin and pretend to shoot them with this rifle." He whipped it off his shoulder, narrowly missing Rose's ear. "Only I get shot first and fall dead, and you drag me back into the cabin."

Rose groaned. Why hadn't Mr. Frontier given *her* a rifle? She was tired of being carried off by the Sioux like some helpless baby.

"It's time, Miss Rose, Oliver. You two git in these trunks," one of the roustabouts said as he lifted the lids of two trunks sitting by the white railing.

Oliver's jaw dropped. "Why are we getting in those?"

"We get carried onstage in the trunks," Rose explained as she climbed into one. "That way the audience won't see us." Lying down, she curled on her side. When the trunk lid lowered, she closed her eyes against the dark.

She could feel the trunk being lifted and carried. When it was finally set down, someone rapped on the top and she pushed open the lid. She was alone inside the small, dark cabin. A second trunk sat next to hers.

Slowly, the lid creaked open. "Is it time to come out?" Oliver's hair was tousled, and he swallowed nervously.

"Yes," Rose whispered as she climbed from her trunk. "After Mr. Pearson announces the act, Annabel will come skipping toward the cabin like she's been gathering berries in the field. When the Indians whoop, she'll scream and shout for us to hide."

"Ladies and gentlemen," Mr. Pearson announced, his deep voice ringing across the grounds. "Celebrating the courageous spirit of our forefathers, Levi Frontier's Wild West presents 'Raid on the Homesteaders' Cabin'!"

Rose helped Oliver from his trunk and straightened her
bonnet. She could hear Annabel singing as she skipped onto
the infield. Suddenly, a war cry cut Annabel off, and right
on cue, she screamed and hollered, "Run! Hide! Indians!"

Oliver clutched Rose's arm. "That sounded real. Are
you sure Annabel's acting?"

Rose nodded, but goose bumps prickled her arms.
Annabel's scream *did* sound unusually real.

Peeking out the window, Rose saw Annabel racing
toward the cabin, the basket bouncing on her arm.
Leaping Elk, a Sioux warrior, his face streaked with paint,
galloped his pony after her. Reaching down, he grabbed
her around the waist and scooped her onto his pony.

Two other Sioux riders galloped around the cabin.
One Feather, Chief White Bear's son, flew past carrying a
flaming torch. Reining his pony to a halt, he touched the
torch to the tree. The dead leaves and branches sizzled,
then grew alive with flames.

Chills ran down Rose's spine. All year, she'd been playing
the homesteaders' daughter. She knew the Sioux warriors
by name—Leaping Elk, One Feather, Hotah. She told herself that this was a show and everyone was acting. But for
the first time, as the war cries filled the air and flames
licked the sky, Rose's heart grew cold with fear.

CHAPTER 5

WHITE BEAR'S SILENCE

"Oliver, what if this *is* real?" Rose whispered as the warriors circled the cabin. "What if the Sioux really are attacking? They'd have every right. Chief White Bear told me how the settlers stole their land. How the cavalry drove them from their sacred places. No wonder he hates men like General Judson."

Did the chief hate him so much he shot him?

Rose shivered. A sharp snap from the burning tree made her jump. "This is only a show . . . only a show," she murmured, trying to still her heart as she got ready to run from the cabin. Finally, she called over her shoulder, "Oliver, they've torched the tree. That's our cue."

When he didn't answer, she turned around. Oliver stood frozen in the middle of the small cabin. The color had drained from his face; the rifle hung by his side.

Rose threw open the door. "Oliver, I'm as scared as you, but we've got to get out there. The audience is waiting!"

"My feet won't move, Rose," Oliver croaked.

Rose took a deep breath. If Oliver proved to be a sissy, Mr. Frontier would never let his son perform again. *I hope you'll understand why I had to do this, Oliver,* Rose thought as she shoved him out the door.

Oliver stumbled into the path of Hotah's pony. Raising his arms, he shielded his head as if expecting a blow. Hotah deftly swerved his pony, plucked the rifle from Oliver's hand, and pointed it at him. Oliver collapsed in a heap.

Thank goodness, he at least managed to die, Rose thought as she darted after him. Grabbing Oliver under the arms, she started to drag him inside. One Feather set the stack of wood on fire, and she could feel the heat on her face.

"Oliver, you could help me out," Rose whispered. "You're dead weight." Oliver's eyelids fluttered, and Rose realized he wasn't pretending to be dead. He'd plumb fainted!

Panting, Rose dropped him just inside the cabin door. A war whoop made her look up. One Feather had jumped off his pony. Tomahawk raised, he advanced toward her, anger distorting his face.

Rose gasped even though she knew this was part of the act. A cry of fear rose in her throat. Frantically, she searched One Feather's eyes for a sign of her friend, but she saw only a stranger behind the streaked paint and fierce expression.

That isn't One Feather, she thought wildly, her imagination fueling her fear. *It's a Sioux warrior avenging the death of his family!* She had to save herself!

With a shrill scream, Rose took off around the cabin. She raced across the infield, her skirts catching her legs, not even slowing at the blast of the cavalry's bugle. When she reached the inside railing, she clambered awkwardly over it. Her skirt ripped and her bonnet flopped across her face. Yanking the bonnet off, she flung it aside as she tore across the dirt track and climbed over the second railing. Behind her, the crowd roared with excitement. Someone called her name, and she felt horse hooves pounding the earth.

Ignoring the call, Rose leaped off the top railing and sprinted toward the campground. When she reached the supply tent, she dove through the door and hid in the shadows behind a wooden box. Holding the stitch in her side, she took deep gulps of air.

When she realized what she'd done, she buried her face in her hands. *What is wrong with you, Rose?* she could hear Mr. Frontier, Zane—*everybody*—ask. *You ruined the show!*

And what *was* wrong with her? Why had she run from One Feather?

Holding her breath, she listened to the sounds outside the tent. Mr. Pearson was announcing the next act. That meant that One Feather, Hotah, and Leaping Elk were riding from the track.

She needed to find them. She needed to apologize for her fear. She needed to look into their faces and remind herself that the raid on the homesteaders' cabin was just part of the show. Above all, she needed to hear that the Sioux had nothing to do with General Judson's shooting.

Checking outside to make sure that no one was around, Rose sneaked from the supply tent, then ran through the campground to the Sioux tipis. The warriors hadn't returned.

She heard chanting from Chief White Bear's tipi. Walking around the smoldering campfire, she went up to the oval-shaped opening. The flap wasn't closed, but she called the chief's name before peering inside. He was sitting cross-legged in the middle of a buffalo hide, his hands resting on his thighs. His heavy eyelids were half-closed. He was dressed for the show in full war paint and eagle-feather headdress. His entrance on Spotted Horse, his Appaloosa, was the Wild West's grand finale.

"Ma-to-sea," Rose asked quietly, "may I come in and speak with you?"

Without opening his eyes, he nodded.

Rose came inside and sat next to him. The tipi was dark, lit only by the glow of the campfire outside. Rose glanced sideways. The chief's lips were moving as he chanted in a low voice. Before every show he steeled himself for the jeers of the white men and women. Once Rose had asked him why he went before the crowd.

"My people" was his only answer.

Later, Zane had explained that White Bear sent the money that Levi Frontier paid him to his people, many of whom were starving on the reservation. Rose had also seen the chief hand pennies to the ragged flower girls and hungry newsboys who hawked their wares outside the show grounds.

"Among the Sioux," Zane had explained to Rose, "it's unthinkable for a man to feed himself while others go hungry. When White Bear sees ragged children begging in the streets, he can't understand it. He also knows that if the white man won't help his own children, he will never help the Indians."

Rose knew that White Bear was wise. Now she hoped he would understand what she was trying to say.

"Ma-to-sea, for the first time, during the show, I was afraid." She pressed her lips together, trying to control the quivering in her voice, and glanced hesitantly up at him.

He bowed his head, letting her know it was okay to continue. She told him about General Judson. She told him about One Feather. She told him about her fear.

"When I ran from the cabin, I didn't know what to think about white people and Sioux. Are we enemies, White Bear?" She gazed sideways at him, needing him to say that he knew nothing about Judson getting shot.

She waited. The fire in front of the tipi glowed red, casting golden flecks on his craggy face. Silently,

White Bear stared straight ahead, his eyes stony.

Sweat broke out on Rose's forehead. All this time, she had thought White Bear was her friend. But were they *really* friends? She knew little of his life before the show, only the few stories he'd told her about the hardships of his people.

She'd heard the audience boo him when he rode onto the show grounds. Mr. Pearson introduced him as a leader and a great chief, but the crowd saw only a warrior who had killed many soldiers.

Now, when Rose studied White Bear's face, she too saw the face of a warrior—a warrior capable of shooting his enemy, General Judson.

Slowly, Rose swallowed. "I'm sorry to plague you with questions, Ma-to-sea," she said. "And I respect your silence."

She crawled from the tipi. Tears rolled down her cheeks. Outside the tent, she stood and took a shaky breath. She had gone to White Bear sure that he would allay her suspicions about the shooting. His silence had only confirmed them.

Rose's head ached as she walked away from the tipis. The campground seemed deserted. Everybody was either performing or watching the show. Rose didn't know what to do. She didn't want to go back to the show. Everyone would ask her why she had run away, and she had no answer.

Empty of people, the tents and tipis looked as dark

and foreboding as caves, and Rose hurried away from them. Stopping, she glanced around, realizing she'd wandered toward the horse barns. The evening air had turned cold, and she shivered. Then she heard a whinny and saw Swift Raven, his head over his stall door. Rose smiled, happy to see him.

As she ran toward the pony, her head cleared. Rose thought about the many times she'd sat with White Bear in his tipi, listening to stories. She'd shared meals with the Sioux and learned riding tricks from White Bear and his sons. In return, her family had given White Bear's family provisions. Mama had tended his sons when they were sick, and Zane had helped the Sioux with such modern-day problems as mail and finances.

"White Bear *is* my friend," Rose told Raven as she slipped into the pony's stall. "If he shot General Judson, he had good reason!"

And even if someone asked her, Rose decided, she would never betray her friend.

Never.

"Rose." Someone shook Rose's shoulder. Her eyes fluttered open. It was dark, and for a second, she didn't know where she was. Then she smelled straw and felt Swift Raven's whiskers tickle her cheek.

I fell asleep in Raven's stall, Rose remembered. Now it was night, and as her eyes adjusted to the dark, she made out a black shape hunched over her like a buzzard.

Rose screamed. Twisting sideways, she scrambled into the corner of the stall.

"Rose!" A strong hand grabbed her wrist. "It's me, Zane."

"Zane?" Relief filled her, and she sagged against the wall. "What are you doing here?"

"What are *you* doing here? We've been hunting everywhere for you. What's wrong? Why'd you run from the cabin like your bonnet was on fire?"

Sitting up, Rose blinked in the dim light. Zane was crouched in front of her, his arms resting on his thighs. His face was shadowed, but she could see the worried expression in his eyes.

"I—I got scared," Rose said hesitantly.

Zane frowned. Taking off his cowboy hat, he laid it on the straw. Then he sat down and relaxed against the wall next to her, his long legs stretched out in front of him. Swift Raven moved closer and lipped at his hat.

Zane swatted at him. "Git on, you fat pony. That's nothing to eat."

Silently, Zane waited for Rose to explain what had happened. Rose knew she could tell her brother about White Bear. He was the only one she could trust.

Finally, she said, "I figured out who shot General Judson. Only I can't tell a soul—excepting you."

Zane cocked his head toward her.

"It was White Bear!"

"White Bear?"

In a rush of words, Rose told Zane everything. She told him about White Bear hating Judson and how, when she confronted the chief in the tipi, he hadn't denied shooting him.

Zane began to chuckle.

"What's so funny?"

"The general's shooting must have muddled your mind."

Rose sat up straighter. "It did not. What I said makes perfect sense. White Bear wanted to avenge his people."

"Rose, if White Bear or any other Sioux wanted to kill General Judson, they wouldn't sneak around and shoot him in the middle of the show. They would face him proudly."

Rose had never thought about that. "Then why didn't White Bear deny it?"

"He was probably too offended. You came crashing into his tipi accusing him of shooting a man."

Rose grimaced. No wonder White Bear had ignored her. She owed him her most humble apology. He was a proud and honest man, and she'd trampled all over his honor.

"Then if it wasn't White Bear, who did shoot the general?"

Zane stuck a stalk of hay in his mouth. "No idea. Had to have been a crack shot, though, to hit a moving target like that."

"Mr. Frontier said the same thing. Did the police find the bullet?" Rose asked.

"I heard they dug one out of the back of the stage-coach." Pulling the stalk from his mouth, Zane pointed it at her. "Close to where you were sitting, Nosy Rose. A little lower, and it might have been *your* ear got shot off."

Rose sucked in her breath, but then she realized Zane was teasing. "Who'd be your assistant, then? That purty auburn-haired gal?"

Zane went silent. Abruptly, he stood and held out his hand. "Come on. Let's get you back to the tent. Mama's frantic."

"What will I say happened?" Rose asked as Zane pulled her to her feet. "I don't want to tell Mama about White Bear."

Zane thought a minute. "Where's your bonnet?"

Rose's hand went to her head. Straw stuck out of her hair. "I lost the darn thing when I ran across the track."

"Let's retrace your flight and find it. We'll singe it in one of the campfires and tell Mama and Levi that you caught it on fire. That's why you ran screaming from the show."

"That's almost the truth," Rose said, shivering as she remembered how she'd run out. "Except it was me that was all afire—with fear!"

CHAPTER 6

ARRESTED!

As soon as Rose woke up the next morning, Mama sat on the edge of her cot and felt her head for fever.

"Mama, I'm fine. Really." Sitting up, Rose wiggled away from Mama's hand. "Like I told you last night, I just got scared when I smelled my bonnet burning."

Mama scrutinized Rose's face. "I don't believe you, Rose Hannah Taylor," she said, smoothing her daughter's hair off her forehead. "I know you too well. A singed bonnet would not send you screaming from the show."

"Then perhaps it was the shock of General Judson getting shot," Rose suggested, repeating Zane's words.

"Perhaps." Mama picked up a brush from her lap and began to comb out Rose's tangled hair. She studied Rose with an anxious frown. "Levi said the general collapsed in your lap. Are you all right? You seem a mite pale."

Rose bit her lip. If she talked about the shooting, Mama

might pry out her silly suspicions about White Bear.

"I'm fine, Mama. Honest. Was the general hurt bad?"

Mama shook her head. "General Judson's head wound will lay him up for a spell, but he's going to be fine. I can't say the same for the Wild West show." She sighed heavily.

"Why? What's wrong?"

"Mayor Reed's closed down the show until the shooter is apprehended. He says the public isn't safe."

"There won't be a show tonight? Why, that's crazy!" Pushing back the quilt, Rose swung her legs to the wood-plank floor. Mama handed her the brush. Rose gave her hair a swipe, then dropped the brush on the cot.

"Mr. Pearson is beside himself." Mama stood and pulled Rose's everyday dress from the trunk. "He says the show needs the revenue to survive."

"Can't we move on to another town?" Rose asked.

"No." Mama furrowed her brow with worry. "The mayor and the chief of police believe the shooter is one of us, so they won't let the show leave, either."

Rose pondered Mama's grave news. Zane had convinced her that neither White Bear nor any other Sioux was the shooter. Who else would have a grudge against the general?

"The mayor's wrong," Rose declared. "No one in the show would have a reason to shoot General Judson."

"I hear he's made enemies because of his political views. But I do believe you're right, Rose. The Wild West folk give more thought to their horses than to politics." Mama sighed as she handed Rose her dress. "In any case, you needn't concern yourself with adult matters. It's late and the mess tent will close any minute, so you'd better hurry off to breakfast."

"I'm powerful hungry, too." Rose slipped into the muslin dress as fast as she could. She didn't dare tell Mama she was hurrying because she wanted to ride Raven. Now that she knew the grownups were looking into the shooting, she could concentrate on her act.

When she had buttoned the last button, she pecked Mama on the cheek and raced from the tent. "Rose, your pinafore and hat!" Mama called, but Rose kept going. Pinafores, hats, and trick riding did not get along.

The mess tent was almost deserted. Only a few late diners sat hunched over their plates, their elbows plopped on the long wooden tables. Rose headed straight for the serving table. Pitchers of milk, a platter of crisp bacon, and a bowl of fried potatoes were on the table. Behind the table, a flat skillet sat on top of one of the huge stoves used to fix victuals for the show folks.

Cook winked at Rose and held up a plate of flapjacks. "Your brother said you'd be late, so I saved 'em jest for you, Miss Rose." He scrutinized her hair. "Thank the Lord, your purty curls didn't ketch fire," he added, pointing a ladle at her head.

Rose winced. Her lie must have spread through camp like a windstorm.

"Thank you, sir," she said when he handed her the plate. She swiped a few sugar cubes from the bowl on the table and stuck them in her dress pocket. When she turned to find a seat, she spotted Oliver huddled in the farthest corner of the tent.

"What's wrong with you?" she asked, sitting on the bench next to him. He was picking at a plate of uneaten flapjacks. "Grub not fancy enough? What do you eat in Boston? *Coddled* eggs?" She giggled as she poured maple syrup from a small pitcher set out on the wooden table.

"Go ahead and tease me, Rose," Oliver said, shoving his plate away. "I can handle it."

"You don't have to be so touchy." Rose forked a huge bite of flapjacks into her mouth, adding between chews, "I'm onwy funnin' wit' you."

Oliver threw his hands in the air. "Except everything you say is true! I *am* lily-livered. I *am* namby-pamby. When I get a chance to prove myself, I turn chicken. It's no wonder Mr. Frontier barely notices me."

Rose swallowed. "Why do you call him Mr. Frontier? He's your pa."

"Except I never see him," Oliver said, sounding miserable. "The few times he does come to Boston, he seems more like a mister than a pa."

"At least you *got* a pa," Rose said, sounding just as dejected. Oliver peered sideways at her, and she grinned. "Aren't we a sorry pair?" she said.

He grinned back at her, pulled his plate toward himself, and polished off his flapjacks.

"Hey, I got an idea," Rose said when they were both finished. "I'll teach you to do a trick on Swift Raven. That'll catch your pa's attention. I'm headed to the barn now."

Oliver wiggled on the bench. "That's thoughtful of you, Rose," he said politely. "I'd love to learn a fancy trick. However, I promised Mr. Pearson I'd type a letter for him."

Rose crooked an eyebrow at him. He dropped his gaze, but she'd already seen the lie in his eyes. "You can't ride a horse, can you?"

His shoulders sagged. "You don't have to make it sound so terrible."

"It's worse than terrible." Grabbing his hand, she pulled him to his feet. "Come on."

"But I don't want to get on a horse," Oliver sputtered as she dragged him from the tent. "They're tall and—and—*hairy,* and once I heard about a man who got trampled under his dray horse's huge feet."

"They're hooves," Rose said, not letting go of Oliver's wrist. Since there was no show tonight, the campground had a lazy air. Menfolk sat around in the sun, whittling, polishing their tack, and cleaning boots. The womenfolk chatted as they hung wash on the line and swept out their tents.

Rose pulled Oliver past two *vaqueros* who sat on overturned buckets, shining their saddles. Pointing at Oliver, the men chuckled at his obvious discomfort.

"Don't you want to impress your pa?" she added.

"Perhaps I can amaze him with my typing."

Rose snorted. "I doubt that'll do it."

When they reached the barn, Oliver was breathless and miserable. As soon as he saw the horses, their heads hanging over the stall doors, he dug in his heels.

"Hey, you two." Zane poked his head from Comanche's stall. "I hope you aren't up to no good."

"I'm going to teach Oliver how to ride," Rose said.

Zane laughed. "That should prove interesting. Oliver," he said, pointing a brush at him, "you listen to Rose. She's the best rider around."

"Okay, Zane. I—I'll try if you say so," Oliver stammered.

Rose stifled a giggle. Oliver was scared. Maybe starting slow would be best—maybe just grooming Raven. She didn't have all day to convince him to mount a horse. There were tricks to practice.

Rose leaned over the door into Comanche's stall. Her brother was brushing the stallion's sleek coat. Comanche bared his teeth at her, but Rose swatted his head away. "Zane, will you help me with the Warrior Stand? I can't quite get the rope the right length."

He nodded. "Warm up your pony first."

"Thank you. I will!" She sprinted to Swift Raven's stall, Oliver trudging behind. "Good morning, Raven!" She kissed the pony's soft muzzle. "This is Oliver. He's going to learn how to brush you."

Raven pricked up his ears and bobbed his head, his black forelock flopping over his bright eyes. Rose fed him the sugar cubes she'd swiped. He crunched them happily, then lifted his lip, showing his teeth. Oliver's cheeks turned white.

"He's just smiling at you, Oliver," Rose said. "Now, let's teach you how to brush a horse. This here's a curry-comb." She thrust it into his hand. "And this here's a brush." Flinging open the door, she pushed Oliver into the stall. He clutched the currycomb to his chest and stared mutely at the pony. Swift Raven ambled over and nuzzled his arm.

"Is he—Is he—Is he—"

"Spit it out," Rose said impatiently as she attacked the manure stains on Raven's side with the brush. "Is he what?"

"Going to eat my shirt?"

"Only if you stand there like a dunce. Move around to his side and start currying him. Like this." She moved the brush in a circular motion.

"I—I can do that. I think." Oliver gulped. Standing as far from Raven as possible, he touched the currycomb against the pony's side. Raven switched his tail. With a yelp, Oliver jumped back into the doorway.

Rose rolled her eyes but didn't stop brushing. Oliver took a deep breath, forced himself to step closer, and began currying harder. In a few minutes, the pony's black coat shone. Rose tacked him up, explaining each piece of equipment to Oliver.

"This here's the bridle. The bit goes in the pony's mouth. The reins attach to the bit. They help steer the pony."

When Raven was ready, Rose led him from the stall, halting him in front of the barn. "Hold him for a second, Oliver," she said, thrusting the reins into his hands.

"But, but—" Oliver sputtered.

Rose backed up until she was behind Raven. Then she ran as fast as she could, plopped her hands on Raven's rump, and leaped over his tail and into the saddle. Her bare feet slid into the stirrups and her skirts bunched around her knees.

Oliver gaped at her. "What was that?"

"The ladylike way of mounting," Rose teased. Reaching down, she took the reins from him. "Thanks for the assistance," she added as she tucked her skirt around her limbs.

"Meet you at the racetrack, Zane!" Rose called as she trotted away from Comanche's stall. Raven had a steady jog and a smooth lope, perfect for performing tricks. She steered the pony through the small gap in the railing and onto the track, where she would practice her tricks. Oliver ran behind to keep up.

Rose squeezed Raven into a canter. As the pony loped down one side of the track, Rose practiced a few easy tricks, showing off for Oliver, who climbed the railing to watch.

Dropping the short reins on the pony's neck, she rode with her arms stretched wide. Then she spun in the saddle, rode backward several strides, and spun back around.

Glancing over her shoulder, she could see Oliver sitting on top of a fence rail, staring open-mouthed at her.

She trotted back and halted Raven in front of Oliver. Raising one hand, she signaled the pony to rear. The pony walked forward a few steps on his hind legs, then dropped down again on all fours.

"See? Nothing to it," Rose said. "Easier than riding one of those newfangled bicycles."

Zane came up, carrying a length of rope. "Ready?"

"Yes, sir." Rose drew up her legs and scooted backward until she was sitting behind the saddle. Zane looped the rope around the pommel, then handed the end to Rose. She stood up, her bare feet planted on Raven's rump.

"How's that feel?" Zane asked.

She leaned back, testing the rope, which helped her keep her balance. "Too long." He wrapped another loop around the pommel and Rose nodded. "Perfect," she said.

"Make sure he's cantering smooth and straight before you stand up," Zane warned.

Rose slipped back into the saddle. "If all goes right, I've got a surprise ending," she added with a secretive grin. As she trotted off, she heard Oliver ask, "She's going to do that when the horse is running?"

Rose trotted Raven past the grandstand and then circled him at the backstretch turn so that they were headed down the straightaway. She squeezed him into a lope. When his rhythm was smooth, she dropped the rein on his neck and scooted behind the saddle again. For a second she sat on Raven's rump, her eyes closed, and let her body feel the rocking motion of his gait. That was the key to riding like a warrior, White Bear had said—to become one with your horse.

Rose held her breath. Suddenly, she felt it. She and Raven were a wild horse racing free across the prairie. Holding onto the rope with her right hand, she grasped the cantle—the back of the saddle—with her left hand, then slowly stood up.

She closed her eyes again, finding her balance. Beneath her bare feet, Raven's muscles rolled and churned as he galloped down the track. She opened her eyes. The wind whipped Rose's skirt, and exhilaration filled her. Raising her left hand in the air, she waved to the imaginary audience in the grandstand.

Zane and Oliver cheered.

Now for the surprise ending. Steadying herself, Rose shortened the rope, then lifted one foot and eased it forward onto the leather seat of the saddle. Then she did the same with the other foot. For a few strides, she rode standing in the saddle, her eyes on Raven's neck to help her keep her balance. As Raven headed for the turn, she dropped down onto the saddle, her skirts fluttering.

"We did it!" Rose whooped as Raven slowed to a trot. "Mr. Frontier's going to *have* to put us in the show."

Grinning, Zane strode across the track toward her.

"We'll call you Trick-Riding Rose. How's that sound?"

"Sounds fine to me." Rose couldn't stop smiling. Halting Raven, she leaned over the pommel and gave him a hug. "How's that sound to you, Raven?"

"Zane." Oliver sidled over, his expression worried. "*Zane.*"

"What's the matter, Oliver? Too much excitement for you?" Rose teased.

"No, look." He gestured toward the gap in the fence. A group of men was striding toward them. Rose recognized Police Chief Whallen, Mayor Reed, and William Pearson. Whallen and the mayor were frowning sternly. Mr. Pearson looked strained. Behind the three men were two uniformed patrol officers.

Rose's grin died. "What's going on?"

"Let me handle it," Zane said. He stepped forward to meet them.

Leaping off Raven, Rose pulled the reins over the pony's head.

"May I help you, gentlemen?" Zane asked.

Without a word, the men surrounded him. Chief Whallen nodded at the two patrolmen, who yanked Zane's arms behind his back and handcuffed his wrists.

"Zane Taylor," the chief of police declared as Rose stared in dumbfounded silence, "you're under arrest for the shooting of General P. Robert Judson."

CHAPTER 7
AN UNEXPECTED ALLY

 *Zane's under arrest!* Thrusting Raven's reins into Oliver's hands, Rose ran over to the men. "Excuse me, Mayor Reed, Mr. Pearson. There must be some mistake!"

Mayor Reed ignored her. Mr. Pearson shot her a warning look. "This is a matter for grownups, Rose," he said in a low voice. "Go tell your mama what's happening."

"The police can't take Zane! They have no cause."

Mr. Pearson strode after the two patrolmen, who were leading Zane toward the black police wagon parked outside the gates. Rose trotted after him. "Mr. Pearson. Sir. You must tell them there's a mistake. Zane wouldn't hurt a flea."

Halting, Mr. Pearson glanced down at her. "*Rose,*" he said sharply, "there's nothing I can do. Go to your mama."

Rose opened her mouth to protest. *How could they take her brother?* Pearson put his hand on her shoulder and spun her so she was facing Oliver. "*Go,*" he repeated.

Rose twisted from his grasp. Up ahead, Zane turned his head and smiled reassuringly. "Don't fret, Rose," he called. "They'll realize their mistake. I'll be home in time to join you in the mess tent for supper."

"Get him inside," the police chief ordered.

The two patrolmen, their hands on Zane's elbows, ushered him to the rear of the black wagon. Zane looked back and winked at Rose, then climbed in.

Tears welled in Rose's eyes. Oliver walked up beside her, still holding onto Raven's reins. "Zane's right," he said. "There must be some mistake."

Rose turned to him. "Run and get your pa, Oliver. Tell him what happened. Tell him he needs to help Zane."

Without a word, Oliver handed her the pony's reins and took off for the campground, his skinny legs pumping.

Clucking to Swift Raven, Rose trotted the pony to the barn. "I'm sorry I can't give you a proper cleaning," she apologized as she untacked him. "But Zane's in trouble." She rubbed his sweaty back with a feed sack, checked his water bucket, then raced back to the tent.

"Mama!" Rose burst through the opening. Mama was sitting in the rocker, a handkerchief pressed to her mouth, her eyes red from weeping. William Pearson stood behind her, his hand on her shoulder as if comforting her.

"You know already?" Rose asked breathlessly.

Mama nodded. "The police came and took Zane's gun box."

Mr. Pearson ran his hand over his bristly muttonchops, his eyes weary. "I'm sorry, Rose. Things don't look good for your brother."

"I don't understand." Rose glanced from Mr. Pearson to Mama, waiting for one of them to say that Zane's arrest was all a mistake.

"Rose, your mama and I need to talk," Mr. Pearson said.

Rose planted her feet and refused to budge.

"Rose Hannah," Mama said in a soft voice, "mind Mr. Pearson."

"Yes, ma'am." Reluctantly, Rose trudged from the tent. As soon as she was out of sight, she raced to the side of the tent. Hoping no one would see her, she knelt in the dirt and lifted the canvas until she could see the hem of Mama's skirt.

"The police found one of Zane's Colts hidden under a tarp in a wagon parked near the grandstand, by the porter's lodge," Pearson was explaining.

One of Zane's revolvers? How could that be? Rose remembered putting the gun box in the tent after Zane's act. And both revolvers had been inside the box. She'd put them there herself!

Breathless, Rose watched Mr. Pearson's boots travel across the wood-plank floor as he paced while talking. "Also, the bullet dug from the stagecoach was the same caliber as the ones Zane uses in his Colts. He's the only one in the show who uses such bullets, Mary Hannah."

"How can this be?" Mama's voice was tearful. "Even if General Judson was shot with Zane's revolver, someone else must have done the shooting. My son had no cause to harm the general."

Rose heard a heavy sigh from Mr. Pearson, and his boots stilled. "General Judson is a well-known war hawk," he said. "For years he's been pushing anti-Indian laws through Congress. Everyone knows that Zane is friends with the Cheyenne and Sioux in the show. The police reason that Zane wanted to stop Judson."

Hogwash! Rose fumed.

"Why, that's hogwash, Mr. Pearson," Mama declared at the same time. Rose heard the rustle of skirts as if Mama had stood up. When she spoke next, her voice was clear and strong. "Zane favors all people. He has no stomach for politics. He certainly had no call to shoot General Judson."

"I'm only telling you what Mayor Reed told me," Pearson said. "You must admit, the evidence is strong against Zane. And he is a crack shot."

"Are you saying you think he's guilty?" Mama asked in a hard voice.

"No, Mary Hannah. You know I'm fond of that boy."

"Then we must do everything to prove his innocence." Suddenly, Mama's skirts swung around in the direction of Rose's hiding place. Rose yanked down the canvas. Holding her breath, she heard Mama's footsteps travel to the back of the tent and stop. A trunk creaked as if it was being opened.

What is she doing? Rose wondered.

"Here. I've saved fifty dollars," Mama said to Mr. Pearson a few minutes later. "It's all I have. I want you to go into Louisville and hire the best lawyer."

"Consider it done. I'll go into town straightaway. Mary Hannah, I'll do everything I can to see that this wrong is made right."

"Thank you, Mr. Pearson."

On hands and knees, Rose crept to the corner of the tent and watched until Mr. Pearson strode away. Rose's thoughts were in a whirl. On one hand, she'd heard enough to know that Zane was in trouble. On the other hand, Zane was innocent. She just knew it. Surely the lawyer Mr. Pearson was going to hire would clear him.

Rose saw Oliver running toward their tent. She sprang to her feet and dusted off her skirt. "Oliver!" she hissed.

He skidded to a halt.

"Did you find your pa?" she pressed. "Did you tell him about Zane?"

Oliver shifted uncomfortably. "Well, I found out where he is. He's in his tent dining with the ladies from the Louisville Women's League. I'll tell him about Zane as soon as he's through entertaining. I promise."

Rose couldn't wait for Oliver's promises. Shooting him an annoyed look, she struck off in the direction of

Mr. Frontier's tent, which was set up in the middle of the campground. When she neared his tent, she spotted Mama striding up the wooden walkway toward the entrance, wearing her best feathered hat and shawl. Rose could hear laughter coming from inside. Mr. Frontier was famous for entertaining high-society visitors and well-heeled dignitaries, keeping them spellbound with his yarns.

Rose joined Mama in front of the opening. "Do you think Mr. Frontier will help Zane?" she whispered.

Mama nodded reassuringly. "He loves Zane like a son. I know he'll want to help." Righting her hat, Mama lifted the tent flap and stepped inside, Rose right behind her.

Standing in the middle of the tent, one foot propped on a wooden box, Mr. Frontier was telling a story to a group of perhaps a dozen well-dressed women and one man. Rose recognized the lone man as Senator North, who'd ridden in the stagecoach last night.

"The sheriff had so many pistols, bowie knives, and rifles slung around his chest," Mr. Frontier was telling the rapt listeners, who were seated on folding chairs and benches, "that when he fell off his horse, he shot himself in the leg and stabbed himself in the arm!"

The audience burst into laughter. When the laughter died down, Mr. Frontier turned his attention to Mama. "What is it, Mary Hannah?" he asked.

"Excuse me for interrupting," Mama said. "I need to speak to you—privately. The matter is urgent."

Mr. Frontier gestured toward the guests. "I'll be with you as soon as these fine ladies have completed their visit. Wait for me at the headquarters tent." His tone was smooth but firm.

"Thank you, sir." Picking up her skirt with one hand, Mama turned and stepped from the tent.

Rose's mouth fell open. This was no time for gracious manners! Zane needed help—*now*!

"Mr. Frontier, sir. Zane's been arrested for shooting General Judson!" she blurted, unable to hold in the news.

A lady gasped and pressed a glove-clad hand to her mouth. Rose looked closely at her and saw that it was the auburn-haired woman.

"I'll speak to your mama about this matter, Rose," Mr. Frontier replied. Turning back to his audience, he started in on another tale as if Rose weren't there. "In 1860, the North Platte area was as wild as a cougar. The buffalo roamed . . ."

For a second, Rose was too stunned to move. Then she spun around and stomped from the tent.

Mama was on the plank walkway outside. "Rose, you had no call to announce our sad news to Louisville society."

Before Rose could reply, she heard a man's voice behind them say, "Excuse me, may I speak with you ladies?" Rose turned to see Senator North stepping from the tent, a bowler hat in his hand.

"I'm sorry to intrude," the senator said when he reached

them. "I'll only take a minute of your time. Did I understand the young lady to say that an arrest has been made
in the shooting of General Judson?"

"Yes!" Rose burst out. "Sir, they've arrested my brother,
Zane Taylor. You saw him perform last night. For some
thickheaded reason, Chief Whallen thinks that *he* shot
General Judson."

The senator glanced at Mama. "Mrs. Taylor, I presume?
You must be terribly distressed. May I ask what evidence
the police have?"

"*Nothing,*" Rose declared. "Except his gun, which—"

"Rose Hannah." Mama placed her hand lightly on Rose's
shoulder. "Let me speak to the gentleman for a moment."

Rose clapped her mouth shut. For a minute, Mama
scrutinized the senator's face. He stood before her, hat
in hand, his gaze direct.

"What is your interest in the situation, Senator North?"
she finally asked. "I realize you were in the stagecoach
when General Judson was shot. However, if I may be so
blunt, that hardly makes you our friend or acquaintance."

"My interest is simply to see that this matter is brought
to a just conclusion," Senator North said. "General Judson
is no friend of mine, but I am horrified that someone
would shoot him in cold blood."

"That someone is *not* my son," Mama declared. "Zane
is being falsely accused, Senator North. The police have
no real evidence."

Senator North nodded. "Perhaps in their haste to catch the shooter, the police did arrest the wrong man. Not only would that be an act of injustice, but it also would leave the real criminal free. For those reasons, I intend to find out the truth and see that justice is served. It would help to know what evidence the police *do* have that pointed them in the direction of your son."

Mama hesitated.

"Tell him," Rose urged. "We need *someone* to listen to us."

"Indeed we do." Mama sighed. As they started walking slowly toward the Taylors' tent, she told the senator about the police finding Zane's revolver in the wagon. "They also claim that the bullet lodged in the stagecoach came from his weapon. Senator North, my son is indeed an excellent shot—but he has no interest in politics. He didn't even know General Judson."

"Mr. Pearson says Zane was arrested because he's a friend of the Sioux," Rose chimed in. "The police think he shot General Judson to keep him from taking away the Indians' lands."

"Ahhh." Senator North nodded. "Now I understand the police chief's reasoning. Judson is actively working with Senator Dawes from Massachusetts to try to push a law through Congress that will take away much of the reservation land given to the Indians."

Rose stopped in her tracks. This was what General Judson and Senator North had been arguing about the night the general was shot. "Why, that's stealing," she said indignantly.

"Some of us in Congress see it that way, too, Rose," Senator North said when they continued walking. "Others, like General Judson, believe the Indians have no rights."

No wonder White Bear hates General Judson, Rose thought.

"Zane is a friend of the Indians," Mama acknowledged. "But he didn't know about Congress aiming to take the Indians' land."

"Unfortunately, Zane's gun is powerful evidence against him, Mrs. Taylor," the senator went on. "But I agree with you; even if his weapon was used, that doesn't prove he pulled the trigger." He paused for a moment, then added, as if talking to himself, "General Judson upset some in Congress and elsewhere because of his outspoken anti-Indian stance. The Wild West performance, with all the shooting and confusion, *could* have given one of them the opportunity to try to kill him."

"Then we need to find that person," Mama said firmly, "since the shooter wasn't my son—*despite* the evidence." When they reached the tent, she put out her hand and smiled gratefully at Senator North. "Thank you for your interest and support, sir."

He took her hand. "I shall do what I can to ensure a thorough investigation. And, please, if there's anything more I can do for you—"

"You can take us to see Zane!" Rose said.

The senator thought a minute, then nodded. "I should be able to arrange that. Tomorrow after breakfast?"

After they decided on the time, the senator left and Mama went inside the tent. Rose sat on the end of the wooden walkway outside the tent and pondered all that had happened.

Like Mama, Rose knew in her heart that Zane wasn't the shooter. And Senator North had mentioned that General Judson had enemies, other enemies besides the Sioux—perhaps an enemy who was a crack shot like Zane?

Rose frowned as another thought struck her: The shooter also had to have known where to find Zane's revolvers. He would have to know that Rose always brought them back to the tent and secured them in the trunk at the foot of Zane's cot as soon as his act was over.

Rose closed her eyes, remembering last night. She'd put the gun box in the tent as always, only . . . Rose choked down a cry . . . *only she'd set the gun box on the sewing table instead of in Zane's trunk!*

Anyone could have sneaked in and taken a revolver! Wrapping her arms around her chest, Rose shivered. Tears filled her eyes. *This was all her fault.*

Her foolish hurrying had gotten Zane thrown in jail!

CHAPTER 8

FALSE FRIENDS

R ose scrambled to her feet. "Mama!" she hollered as she rushed into the tent.

"What?" Mama answered from beside the clothes tree. Her arms were raised as she pulled out her hat pins.

"Last night, after Zane's shooting act, I brought his Colts back here, but I set them on the sewing table. I called to you and then I ran off. I was in a hurry to get back for 'Attack on the Dry Gulch Stage.' Did you put the gun box in Zane's trunk right away?"

Mama stopped fiddling with her hat. "Rose, I wasn't here when you brought the gun box back. I went to see Alma Nelson. She's with child and feeling poorly. I didn't get back until the show was almost over."

"When you got back, where was the gun box?"

Mama's gaze shot to the sewing machine. "Over there. As soon as I returned from Alma's, I locked the box in Zane's trunk. I didn't notice if one of the revolvers was missing. I was in a rush because by then Mr. Frontier had informed me that you'd run off."

Rose moaned. "Then it *is* my fault Zane's in jail. Mama, I left the gun box out in plain sight. Someone must have reached in and stolen one of his revolvers—and then used it to shoot Judson."

"But why would someone do that?" Mama asked. "Unless . . ." A dark cloud crossed her face. "Unless someone deliberately wanted to cast suspicion on Zane. But who? Only someone from the show would know that you bring his gun box back to the tent after his act—" She pressed her fingers to her mouth. "No, not someone from the show. This troupe is our *family*."

Rose caught her breath. What was Mama saying? That someone from the Wild West show really had stolen Zane's gun and shot Judson?

Goose bumps prickled up her arms. "Who else could've taken the Colt, Mama?" Rose asked in a whisper. "Outsiders can't go sneaking around the campground unescorted."

"Rose, we mustn't speak of our suspicions to anyone. We can't trust anyone until we know more. Tomorrow, when we see Zane, we'll need to find some answers."

"Like where he was when General Judson was shot."

"And who knew where he kept his revolvers. Perhaps he told someone who wasn't in the show." Mama pressed her lips together as if to hold back a sob. "Somehow, Rose, we have to find the truth."

Rose wrapped her arms around Mama's waist. She hated to see her so sad. "We'll find a way to set Zane free, Mama. Don't worry."

☙

"All ready, ladies?" Senator North asked after he greeted Rose and Mama the next morning. "I've hired a carriage for the ride into town."

"Yes, sir," Rose said. She was wearing a clean calico dress, pressed pinafore, and *shoes.* As she walked from the tent, she wiggled her toes to relieve a cramp. Mama followed, carrying a basket that Cook had packed for Zane with bacon and bread, doughnuts, and an apple pie. Rose had added a warm shirt and a four-leaf clover for luck.

Mama was dressed in a short jacket, high-necked white blouse, and striped skirt, her hair swept under a brimless hat called a toque. Rose knew her outfit was not the latest fashion, but she still thought Mama looked beautiful.

When they passed the headquarters tent, Oliver ran out to meet them. He handed Mama a *Popular Science* magazine. "Give this to Zane. It's the latest issue. I know he wanted to read it. Tell him there's a story on motorcars."

"Thank you, Oliver." Mama tucked the magazine in the basket. "He'll appreciate your thoughtfulness."

As the trio walked through the campground, Rose glanced right and left. Many of their friends in the troupe had called on Mama when they heard about Zane's arrest. But now the cowboys, horse handlers, and cooks suddenly seemed suspicious. Which of them had a reason to shoot General Judson? Was it Billy Dees? He was a crack shot. Where was *he* during the attack on the Dry Gulch Stage?

"This way, Rose." Senator North's voice interrupted her thoughts. He was gesturing toward a carriage, pulled by a team of perfectly matched horses, that waited just beyond the grandstand. The horses' chestnut coats gleamed as brightly as the brass on their harnesses.

Rose patted the offside horse, who was twitching his lower lip and rolling his eyes. *No wonder he's miserable,* Rose thought. The driver had the checkreins pulled so tight that the horses' necks were arched unnaturally.

Zane loved animals as much as Rose. She knew what her brother would do if he were here. "Sir," Rose called up to the coachman. "Your team would perform better if you undid that murderous checkrein."

The coachman only grunted. Senator North came up beside Rose. "The lady is correct," he said. He pulled a gold coin from his pocket and flicked it up to the coachman.

"Yes, sir." Touching his hat with his whip, the coachman jumped down and began to adjust the reins.

North extended his elbow to Rose. "Miss Taylor, may I help you into the cab?"

"Why, certainly, Senator," Rose said just as politely.

Minutes later, they were headed into Louisville. Rose

pushed aside the curtain and peered out the window. Even though her mind was on Zane, she couldn't help but wonder at the sights as the horses trotted along the dirt road. They passed a wagon sprinkling water on the dusty city streets, and delivery wagons with signs such as *Louisville Pie Company* and *Singer Sewing Machines* written on the side.

"The city has over one hundred thousand citizens," Senator North remarked as the carriage rolled into the busy downtown. He pointed out the window. "Yonder is Macauley's Theatre, and over there is City Hall."

Rose marveled at the huge brick buildings with stately columns, balconies, and towers. The sidewalks were filled with shoppers on this sunny Saturday morning. Carriages, wagons, and hansom cabs rattled along the streets. Vendors and peddlers strolled everywhere. A Negro woman stood by a cart, hollering, "Hot corn! Yellow and sweet!" A bootblack carried his box from carriage to carriage, crying, "Shine 'em! Make 'em shine!"

Although the Wild West had played up and down the East Coast, the show rarely stayed long enough in one place for Rose to visit the towns. If she hadn't been on such a serious mission, she would have been delirious with the sights.

"Louisville even has one of the first teams in baseball's new National League," Senator North added.

"You sound proud of your city," Mama said. She'd been quiet the entire ride.

"Yes, ma'am, I am—which is one reason I aim to get to

the bottom of this shooting. If Chief Whallen has arrested
the wrong man, then my city needs to make it right."

The carriage halted in front of a two-story redbrick
building. Moments later, the coachman opened the door.
"City jail," he announced.

Senator North climbed out and helped Rose and her
mother. "Wait for us," he said, pressing another coin into
the coachman's palm.

For a moment, Rose stood with Mama on the sidewalk,
looking up at the building. Two glass-paned windows
stretched tall on either side of the wide doorway. They
were covered with steel bars.

Rose's stomach fluttered. She'd never been inside a
jailhouse before. Would Zane be locked in a tiny cell?
Would he be chained up? Housed with murderers?

As Senator North escorted them up the steps, Rose
reached for Mama's hand. They stepped through the
double doors into a high-ceilinged room. Benches lined
the bare, whitewashed walls. In the middle of the room,
a burly man in a navy blue uniform manned a wooden desk.
"May I help you, sir?" he asked Senator North.

"We're here to see a prisoner, Zane Taylor," the senator said.

Rose peered around the officer. Behind him, an open
door revealed a hall that she guessed led to the jail cells.

"You may see him, sir. The ladies must wait out here."
The officer nodded toward one of the benches.

"But he's my brother," Rose protested.

"Jailhouse rules. No ladies allowed in the cells."

Rose glanced up at Mama, who had a pinched look on her face. "Senator North, would you be kind enough to take this basket in to Zane?"

As Mama handed him the basket, she whispered, "Sir, can we also trust you to ask Zane some questions?"

"Yes, ma'am," Senator North replied. As he led Mama away from the desk to talk in private, Rose heard him say quietly, "I have some questions of my own, Mrs. Taylor. I hope to get to the bottom of this, just as you and your daughter do."

Rose strained to hear their whispered conversation, but their words were drowned out as two patrolmen barged through the front door, dragging a struggling, swearing man wearing leg irons. His hair was tangled, and he smelled like an outhouse. When the patrolmen hauled him past Rose, he leered at her, showing off rotten teeth.

Rose recoiled as he was dragged through the door that led to the hallway. If that's what a real varmint looked like, she'd take Con Hardy and his gang any day.

"Rose," Mama said softly.

Rose started. She turned to find Mama standing alone beside her. Senator North was striding through the doorway after the patrolmen.

"Let's wait on the bench."

Rose followed Mama and sat down beside her. "Do

you think Senator North will find out where Zane was when the general was shot?" she asked.

Mama smoothed her striped skirts, then folded her hands in her lap. "We can hope."

"Do you think he'll get Zane freed?"

Mama patted Rose's hand. "Not today. But surely Mr. Pearson has found a good lawyer. If so, Zane may be home soon. Now sit quiet. The senator may take a while."

As they waited, Rose squirmed on the hard bench, wishing she were talking to Zane. She missed him so! "Do you think he'll like the pie and doughnuts Cook packed?" she asked Mama. "And the warm shirt?"

"Yes. Now hush," Mama scolded. "You're in a public building. This is a good time to practice being a lady."

Rose blew out her breath. As far as she was concerned, there was *no* good time to be a lady. If she were wearing trousers, she'd be visiting her brother now instead of sitting on a hard seat.

Twenty minutes later, Senator North strode from the hall with the empty basket. Rose popped off the bench. Mama stood up too, an expectant expression on her face.

"Let's talk outside." The senator took Mama's arm and escorted her outside. Rose hurried after them. At the bottom of the steps, North turned to face Rose and Mama.

"Zane thanks you for the food," he said, "and for the flannel shirt. The cell is cold at night. He says to tell you he misses you both and wishes he could see you."

"Did he say anything about the lawyer Mr. Pearson engaged for him?" Mama asked.

Senator North shook his head, his expression grave. "No, I was his first visitor."

Mama's brows rose. "Why, yesterday I gave Mr. Pearson money to hire a lawyer!"

"Perhaps Mr. Pearson did, and the lawyer just hasn't been by. The good news is that Zane swears he wasn't near the grandstand when General Judson was shot."

"Can he prove where he was?" Rose asked.

Senator North paused. "I believe that's a problem. Zane says he's honor-bound not to tell who he was with."

"Even if it means he stays in jail?" Mama asked.

"It seems he's protecting someone," the senator replied. "Do you have any idea who he might have been with?"

Rose thought back to that night. After Zane's shooting performance, she'd teased him about the handkerchief. He had left abruptly, saying, "I have to meet a lady."

"Mama, I think I know where Zane was when General Judson was shot. With a lady."

"Then why won't he tell the police?" Mama declared. "It would clear him of this grievous error."

Senator North cleared his throat. "I suspect he's protecting the lady's virtue."

"What foolishness!" Mama's eyes flared with anger. "Who will protect him from prison? Does my son even realize what deep trouble he's in?"

"I'm not sure," Senator North said. "When I told him about the police finding his Colt under the tarp in the wagon, he seemed genuinely surprised."

"Did you ask him who might have known his Colts were kept in the tent?" Rose interrupted.

"He said as far as he knows, only show folk know that."

Mama cut her eyes to Rose. Rose guessed what she was thinking. *The shooter had to be someone from the Wild West!*

"I know it seems grim," Senator North said, taking Mama's arm and leading her toward the carriage. "But we mustn't give up."

Rose followed them down the walkway. While Senator North helped her mother into the carriage, Rose stepped into the street and stroked the two horses.

Nearby, a hansom cab slowed. A pretty young woman was looking out the window, her gaze fixed on the jail. Rose caught her breath. It was the auburn-haired lady!

"Wait!" Rose dashed toward the cab. "I must speak with you!"

When the lady saw Rose, her cheeks paled. "Drive on!" she called to the coachman. Rose grabbed for the door handle just as the driver whipped the horses. The cab lurched out of reach.

Heartsick, Rose watched the carriage careen around the street corner, disappearing with the only person who could free her brother from jail.

CHAPTER 9

DISCOVERIES

Mama and Senator North hurried to the other side of the carriage. "Rose Hannah! What in the world are you doing?" Mama cried. "You could have been run over!"

Rose pointed up the street. "The lady—the one Zane was with that night—I saw her inside that cab!"

Senator North stared up the busy street as the cab disappeared from sight. "Are you certain it was the same lady?"

Rose told him about Zane meeting the lady for the first time as he practiced on the track. "He was smitten right then, I could tell. Later, she was in the audience during his shooting act. Yesterday, I saw her again when Mr. Frontier was entertaining the Louisville Women's League. I'd know her anywhere."

"Perhaps she was coming to the jail to see Zane." Mama furrowed her forehead in thought. "If only we can find out who she is and persuade her to help."

An idea popped into Rose's head. "The handkerchief! After Zane's act that night, she threw him her handkerchief. Perhaps her name's embroidered on it. Perhaps he put it in his trunk."

Senator North nodded. "I think you ladies are on the right track. I must stay in town, but the carriage will take you back to the show grounds. In the meantime, I'll see if I can find out about that lawyer for Zane."

"Thank you, Senator North," Mama said. "You have been very kind."

When they were seated in the carriage and headed back to the racetrack, Rose said, "Senator North is nice, but do you think he'll be able to help us?"

Mama sighed. "I hope so, Rose Hannah. At this point, we have no one else."

An hour later, Rose was in their tent kneeling next to Zane's trunk. Mama had stopped off at the headquarters tent in hopes of finding Mr. Frontier or Mr. Pearson. Rose couldn't wait.

As she swung back the trunk lid, Rose told herself it was all right to snoop. After all, she was trying to prove her brother's innocence.

Heart thumping, she began to root through Zane's belongings. Under his woolen drawers, she found a photo of Zane with Papa. She held it up to the light, marveling at how much Zane had grown to look like his father. Digging further, she found photos and postcards from young ladies named Lila, Lenore, and Sarah, a lock of blond hair, a silk stocking, and a lacy garter. But no handkerchief.

Rose sat back on her heels. *Perhaps the auburn-haired lady wasn't special after all.*

No, that didn't make sense. If Zane had no feelings for her, he would have told the police her name.

Pondering, Rose sat on her brother's cot. A tattered quilt covered it. Tucked under the pillow was a Bible. She pulled it out. Something was stuck inside, separating the pages. When she opened the book, a lacy white handkerchief fluttered onto the cot. Rose lifted it to her nose. Lily of the valley. It had to be the auburn-haired lady's.

Rose unfolded the handkerchief. In one corner were the initials ABR embroidered in violet thread.

ABR. Rose frowned. How could she find out who those initials belonged to?

Rose pictured Zane's sweetheart sitting with the Louisville Women's League in Mr. Frontier's tent, listening to his yarns. She knew Mr. Pearson kept lists of the guests who toured the grounds so he could contact them again for donations and publicity. If he had a list for the Women's League, maybe Rose could match the initials to a name.

And she knew just how to get that list without Mr. Pearson knowing—*Oliver.*

She found Oliver sitting under a tree beside his father's tent, his nose in a *Bicycle World* magazine, a straw hat on his head. "Look at this, Rose." Holding up the magazine, he pointed to a photo of a woman astride a bicycle wearing an odd outfit, a calf-length skirt split into two, like pants.

Rose took the magazine from him and read out loud, "'Bloomers — the modern outfit for the lady cyclist.' Why, that's what I need for trick riding!" she exclaimed. "Then my skirts wouldn't be flying every which way showing off my—" Just in time, she stopped herself from saying "nether garments," but Oliver flushed bright red anyway.

Smiling winsomely, Rose stuck the magazine behind her back. "Oliver, I need your help."

"My help?" Oliver pushed his glasses up his nose.

"I need to look at the lists of visitors' names that Mr. Pearson keeps."

He gave her a suspicious look.

"I bet you've seen them on his desk when you're doing his typing." When Oliver didn't budge, Rose added, "I'm particularly interested in the ladies who visited Mr. Frontier yesterday. It will help get Zane out of jail."

"Well, why didn't you say so? I'll do anything to help Zane." Oliver jumped to his feet. "I typed that list myself. It's got to be in one of those stacks on Mr. Pearson's desk."

Rose handed him his magazine, and the two hurried to the headquarters tent. Slowly, Rose approached the open door and peered inside. The tent was empty.

"I'm going in," Rose said. "You keep watch. Whistle if you see Mr. Pearson or your father coming."

"Check." Oliver sat cross-legged on the wooden walkway in front of the tent and opened his magazine. Rose hurried over to Mr. Pearson's rolltop desk. Papers were stacked in hodgepodge piles on the desktop. Some stuck out from the cubbyholes. Oliver had said the list for the Louisville Women's League was in one of the stacks. But which one?

Beads of sweat broke out on Rose's forehead. She'd never find it!

Quickly, she began rifling through the papers, scanning each typewritten sheet. Some of the words were too hard for her to read. Others were easy: *Train Schedule, Louisville Reporters, Feed Bills.* Halfway through the second pile, she caught sight of a newspaper clipping. She almost flipped past it, but the word "Dawes" in the headline gave her pause. She sounded out the rest of the headline: "Dawes A-lot-ment Act."

Rose remembered Senator North telling her and Mama about General Judson working with Senator Dawes. The two men were trying to get a bill passed that would take the Indians' lands. Glancing at the article, she saw that it contained a list of congressmen who were against the bill. One name was circled. *Senator North.*

Rose knew Senator North was against the bill. He'd made no secret of it—that's why he and General Judson argued so—but why was Mr. Pearson interested?

Rose stiffened at a noise outside the tent. *Freet. Fweep.*
Her heart pounded. Was that a whistle? She heard a louder
freep. That *had* to be a warning. Someone was coming!

Pulse racing, Rose leafed through the last stack. When
she saw a sheet with the words "Louisville Women's
League" typed at the top, she stuffed it into the pocket
of her pinafore and darted outside.

Oliver was standing by the tent opening, his lips puck-
ered in a whistle. His father and Mr. Pearson were heading
toward the tent, deep in conversation. Rose dove behind
a rain barrel by the corner of the tent, dragging Oliver
with her. They huddled against the wooden staves, listening as the two men drew closer.

"I want my money," Mr. Pearson said in a gruff voice.

"You know I don't have that kind of cash handy."
Mr. Frontier's tone was cajoling.

"Then *raise* it. I want my money before the show folds."

Rose sucked in her breath. What did Mr. Pearson mean?

"The Wild West is not going under," Mr. Frontier said.
"Now that Zane is in jail, the mayor's letting the show go
on. The grandstand will be packed tonight. Everyone will
want to see where the notorious shooting took place."

"Levi, you're a fool. One packed night won't get the
show out of the red."

Rose peeked around the barrel. Mr. Pearson was jab-
bing a finger at Mr. Frontier's chest. "For the last time,
I want my money," he declared before striding off.

Rose heard Mr. Frontier mutter something under his breath, and then he ducked into the headquarters tent. When both men were gone, she collapsed against the barrel. "What was that all about?" she asked Oliver, keeping her voice low. "I've never seen Mr. Pearson so angry. Is the show really going to fold?"

Oliver dropped his gaze. "I shouldn't tell."

Sitting upright, Rose glared at him. "Oliver Farley, you'd better tell me what's going on, or one night when you're sliding into bed, you'll find a rattler under your quilt."

Oliver blanched. "All right, I'll tell you. Last night, Mr. Pearson came to our tent and told Mr. Frontier that he wants to sell his half of the Wild West. Not only does he want to get out of show business, he has a chance to buy a ranch dirt-cheap in South Dakota. He kept saying that the show was in debt and that it may have to fold."

"What did your pa say?" Rose asked.

"Mr. Frontier argued that the show is a hit and just needs a few more towns to break even—but he did sound worried. When Mr. Pearson insisted on his money, Mr. Frontier said he just didn't have the cash to buy him out." With a sigh, Oliver added, "My father is no businessman. He only knows how to spin yarns and ride a horse."

Rose bit her lip, wondering if anything she'd learned would help Zane. Both Levi Frontier and William Pearson needed money, but she didn't see what that had to do with her brother. Only one thing was certain—neither man gave a hoot about Zane. Frontier was only worried about the show going on. Pearson was only interested in money. She'd bet he hadn't spent Mama's fifty dollars on a lawyer.

Anger made her stomach churn. All this time, she'd thought the two men cared about her family. Now she knew better, and it was as bitter to swallow as Dr. Benjamin's Tonic.

"Rose, promise you won't tell anyone what I told you," Oliver said.

"I won't tell, Oliver. But if the show folds, Mama and me are in powerful trouble. This has been our home for years." She sighed.

"I'm sorry, Rose." Oliver sighed, too. "I wish there were something I could do." Then his eyes widened. "Hey, did you find the name of the mysterious lady?"

"Oh, my!" Rose had forgotten all about her mission. She dug the crumpled paper from her pocket and scanned the list of Louisville ladies. Her gaze lit on the only name that matched the initials ABR: *Abigail Booker Reed.*

Rose's breath caught in her throat. She pictured Mayor Reed's wife sitting across from her in the stagecoach after General Judson had been shot. "You were very brave," she'd told Rose. "Braver than my daughter Abigail would have been under such trying circumstances."

No wonder Zane wouldn't reveal the identity of his auburn-haired sweetheart. She was the mayor's daughter!

CHAPTER 10

TURNED AWAY

Rose let out a groan.
"What is it?" Oliver asked. "Did you find out who's the mysterious lady?"

"I do believe she's Mayor Reed's daughter."

Oliver's jaw dropped. "The mayor's daughter—with a *cowboy*?"

Rose poked him hard in the chest. "Are you saying Zane's not worthy of her? I'd say *she's* not worthy. Especially if she's too stuck on herself to come to my brother's aid." Furious, she scrambled to her feet. "I've got to tell Mama." She headed for her tent at a run.

Mama was hunched over the sewing machine, her feet furiously pumping the treadle. Rose could tell by her intent manner that something was wrong.

"You talked to Mr. Pearson, Mama?"

Mama shook her head. "He was too *busy* to see me."

"I bet he wasn't too busy to spend your lawyer money." Rose told Mama about the conversation she'd overheard.

Mama's feet stopped pumping. "They aren't concerned one whit about Zane!" she said angrily.

Rose agreed. "At least me and Oliver have some news."

"Zane's mysterious sweetheart is the mayor's daughter!" Oliver announced from the doorway, his straw hat in his hands. Mama's eyes widened at the news.

"Now that we know who she is, we've got to convince her to help Zane," Rose said.

Mama pushed her chair away from the sewing machine. "Yes. We'll have to find out where she lives and pay a call."

"The Reeds *must* live in Louisville." Rose pulled her murderous shoes from the corner where she'd thrown them earlier. Then she rushed to her trunk to find clean stockings.

"Rose, slow down," Mama cautioned. "Louisville is a big city. We don't know our way around."

Rose spun to face her. "We can't let that keep us from saving Zane!" she protested.

Oliver cleared his throat. "I-I'll be your escort."

Rose stared at him. He flushed and twirled his hat in his hand. "I'd be honored. I may not be able to ride a horse, but I know all about getting around cities."

"There. It's settled," Rose told Mama. "We'll leave right away." Opening her trunk, she plucked out stockings.

"We accept your offer, Oliver. But we'll leave in the morning," Mama decided.

"But what about Zane?" Rose fumed. "He may be bunking with murderers!"

"My mind is made up, Rose Hannah. We're not traipsing around Louisville in the dark. It's too dangerous." Mama sat down again at the sewing machine, and immediately it started to whir and hum.

Rose sighed. She had to admit that Mama was right. "Tomorrow morning, then. First thing. Oh, I just hope Zane can wait one more night!"

The next morning, Oliver led Rose and Mama to a tiny station outside the grandstand to wait for the mule trolley to Louisville. The sun was still low in the east, but the day promised to be warm and clear.

Rose stepped onto the wooden platform and peered anxiously down the metal tracks.

"A trolley arrives every half hour," Oliver announced. He checked his pocket watch. "It'll be here in ten minutes."

Rose's brows lifted under her straw hat. "How do *you* know all about the trolley?"

"The first day I arrived, I took the trolley into town to see the Southern Exposition." His eyes lit up. "Thomas Edison's incandescent bulb was on display. What a miracle!"

Rose snorted. "Who needs electric light when you got kerosene and gaslight?"

"*Be* a naysayer, Rose. I predict it'll be one of the greatest inventions in history."

In ten minutes exactly, Rose spotted two mules pulling the trolley car up the tracks. The car looked like a long wagon with a flat roof, open windows, and metal wheels. A man in a black uniform stood on a platform at the front of the trolley, holding the reins. When the mules halted, the man hollered, "Last stop, Louisville Jockey Club! End of the line! All aboard for the city of Louisville!"

"That's the conductor," Oliver explained as he climbed onto the trolley and paid the fare for all of them. Rose watched the three nickels drop into a little chute and roll into the fare box. Then she walked down the narrow aisle between the wooden seats and slid into the seat behind Oliver. Mama sat down next to her.

The conductor clucked, and the mules pulled the trolley around the station and down the tracks in the direction they'd come.

"The night of the Wild West show, the trolley was so full that passengers were hanging off the sides," Oliver told Rose and Mama. "The city built this line just to bring audiences to the racetrack."

"That's all fine information, Oliver, but we have to determine how we're going to find the mayor's residence," Mama said. "The city's a mite large for us to be knocking on every door."

"Leave that to me." Sliding from his seat, Oliver went up to the conductor and slipped a coin from the pocket of his knickers.

"Just like Senator North," Rose whispered to Mama. "From now on, *I'm* carrying coins. Next time we go to the jail, I'll bribe the jailer to let us see Zane."

"You'll do no such thing, Rose Hannah," Mama whispered back. "That is not proper behavior for a lady."

Rose rolled her eyes. One day she'd like to know what ladies *were* allowed to do. The list seemed dang short.

Mama patted Rose's hand. "Besides, next time we go to the city jail, it will be to free Zane. I'm sure of it."

Mama's confidence made Rose smile.

"It's all taken care of," Oliver said when he came back to the seat. "The conductor says the trolley stops in the mayor's neighborhood."

"Why, that's wonderful news," Mama said. "Thank you, Oliver."

For a second, Rose eyed Oliver with a touch of what *might* amount to respect. Perhaps riding a horse wasn't the only important skill in life.

They traveled through town, a variety of passengers climbing on and off. Finally the conductor hollered, "Cave Hill Cemetery. Cherokee Triangle. End of the line!" He halted the team at a stop right in front of a cemetery. A group of housemaids wearing lightweight shawls waited to board, carrying baskets on their arms as if they were headed into town to shop.

Rose stood and followed Oliver and Mama down the aisle. "The conductor says Mayor Reed lives on Slaughter

Avenue." Oliver pointed up the street, past the rows of marble gravestones. "Fifth house on the left."

He pressed another coin into the conductor's palm before getting off. "Thank you for your trouble, sir."

As the three walked down the red-clay street, Rose suddenly felt apprehensive. Wrought-iron fences surrounded the stately homes and their manicured lawns and flower gardens. The carriage houses and stables behind the homes were ten times as big as her family's tent.

Oliver walked jauntily beside her. "This looks like my neighborhood in Boston. Oh, how I miss it!"

"You live in a mansion?" Rose asked.

"Well, I guess you could call it a mansion." He pointed to a three-story house with dormers. "Ours looks a little like that one."

Ahead of them, Mama stopped in front of an iron gate. "This is it. The fifth house on the left."

Rose gulped. The mayor's house was a fancy brick mansion with white columns. "What are we going to say?"

Mama adjusted her jacket and squared her shoulders. "We've come this far. I pray that the right words will find me." Tipping her chin, she marched up the brick walkway, climbed the marble steps to the front porch, and knocked on the door. Rose had never seen Mama so determined. She followed behind, her head tilted just as high. Oliver stayed by the gate.

A manservant with snow-white hair and wrinkled brown

skin opened the door. His gaze swept over them. "Yes?" he said in a disdainful voice.

"My name is Mary Hannah Taylor. I'd like to speak to Miss Abigail Reed."

The servant frowned. "I'm sorry. Miss Reed is not receiving visitors today."

"This is an important matter," Mama persisted. "If you'd be kind enough to inform Miss Reed that we're here, I'm sure she'd—"

"Good day, madam," the servant said. Then he shut the door in her face.

"Wait! You don't understand how important this is!" Rose knocked and called, "Tell Miss Abigail we need to speak to her about my brother! Her sweetheart!"

"Rose." Mama put her hand on Rose's wrist. "We will not act like ruffians."

"But it's not fair." Rose felt tears threatening. "We came all this way. He didn't even hear what we had to say."

Gently, Mama turned her around and held her close. "We'll find another way," she said, her voice weary.

Arms around each other, they walked down the sidewalk toward Oliver.

"*Psst.* Miss. Excuse me, *Miss,*" a voice hissed somewhere behind them.

Rose swung around. A girl wearing a starched apron and white cap waved at her from behind a bush at the corner of the house.

Rose hurried across the grass. The girl's eyes darted nervously to the front door. Then she whispered, "My mistress, Miss Abigail, sends you her heartfelt apologies. Her father discovered she'd attempted to go to the jail yesterday. Now he's keeping her prisoner in her bedroom." She pointed to an upstairs window.

"Tell Miss Abigail that my brother's freedom depends on her!"

The girl shook her head. "She wants to help, but she cannot. Her father is watching her like a hawk. He says that he won't allow her name to be associated with a *cowboy* and a suspected *criminal*—that her reputation and honor would be tarnished forever!"

A footstep sounded on the front porch. The girl blurted, "I must go!" and in a flash, she disappeared around the side of the house.

The servant hobbled onto the porch wielding a cane. "You!" he bellowed at Rose. "Get away from this residence!"

"Hurry, Rose!" Oliver gestured to her from the gate. Behind him, Mama stood with her hands clasped over her mouth. Rose raced across the lawn and darted through the gate. As Oliver shut it behind her, Rose turned to look at the house. In an upstairs window, someone drew back a curtain, and Rose caught a shadowy glimpse of the auburn-haired lady.

CHAPTER 11

A STORM OF QUESTIONS

The whole ride home on the trolley, Rose's head ached from the noon heat and the dust kicked up by the mules. Beside her, Mama swayed quietly on the wooden seat. Her usually neat hair straggled from under her toque. Her hands were clenched in her lap. Rose could tell her determination had run dry.

Abigail Reed had been their only chance to free Zane. Who would help them now?

Not Frontier and Pearson. They were concerned only with themselves. Senator North? Rose guessed he had many other matters to attend to.

"Patterson and Vine!" the conductor called.

Rose looked up, recognizing the busy intersection from their trip to the jail yesterday. When the trolley stopped, Oliver hopped off and disappeared into the throng.

"Where's he going?" Rose asked, alarmed.

Minutes later, the trolley started moving. Rose leaned out the open window and searched for Oliver. Suddenly, he dashed from the crowd, ran alongside the trolley, and jumped on board. His pockets bulged. "I figured you ladies had to be as hungry as I." He handed them each a steaming-hot sweet potato and a rosy red apple. Then he tipped his cap, pulled a daisy from under it, and handed it to Mama. "To say I'm sorry, Mrs. Taylor. About everything."

"Thank you, Oliver," Mama said. "You've done everything you could to help."

As Rose bit hungrily into the apple, she vowed never again to tease Oliver. She would have thanked him, but the trolley was full and he went to stand up front. She could hear him chattering to the conductor about Thomas Edison's electric lights.

By the time Rose had polished off the apple and sweet potato, her head had cleared. "Mama, we can't let this setback sway our determination to free Zane."

Mama sighed. "Of course not, Rose. But there's a show tonight, and I have costumes to mend."

Rose brushed potato crumbs off her lap. "Then I'll carry on alone. I won't need to assist Zane tonight. And Mr. Frontier"—she spat out the name bitterly—"can find another settlers' daughter."

"Rose," Mama said, taking her hand. "Don't be foolhardy. Our livelihood now depends entirely on Mr. Frontier's

goodwill. If Zane is no longer in the show, Mr. Frontier
could ask us to leave."

Rose could only stare at Mama. Their family had been
with the show since the early days when it struggled to find
an audience. Would Mr. Frontier dismiss them that easily?

Yes, she realized. *Hasn't he dismissed Zane without a
thought?*

Mama squeezed Rose's fingers. "We'd have nowhere
to go. That's why I need to make myself invaluable as a
seamstress. That's why you need to please him. Do you
understand?"

"Yes, ma'am. I understand." Rose's voice came out a
whisper, and she huddled against Mama, realizing that
they were truly alone.

Later that afternoon, Rose was in Raven's stall. She'd
spent the noon meal pondering how to help Zane but had
come up dry. Finally, she decided to ride Raven, hoping the
wind whistling past her ears would clear her brain.

She was cinching the pony's saddle when a dark shadow
fell over her. Swift Raven nickered, and Rose whipped
around. White Bear stood in the doorway of the stall.
Dressed in a calico shirt and deerskin leggings and with
his hair in long plaits, he didn't look quite as formidable
as when he wore his headdress and war paint.

Rose hadn't seen the chief since she'd confessed her
fear to him. For a second, she was tongue-tied.

"Rose," the chief said. "Are you riding like a Sioux?"

"I've been practicing what you taught me, Ma-to-sea,"
Rose said as she led Raven from the stall. "But I still need
help. Especially since *Zane* isn't here." She emphasized
Zane's name, then watched the chief out of the corner
of her eye. He only nodded.

He has to know that Zane's in jail, Rose thought as she
led Raven toward the track. *Is that why he's here?*

As White Bear walked beside her, she glanced sideways
at him, wanting to ask if he knew about Zane. Her brother
was a friend of White Bear's. But as long as she'd known
the chief, he'd been purposely silent when discussion
turned to "white men's problems."

"I especially need help with the Warrior Mount,
Ma-to-sea. Raven is the perfect warrior's pony," she said,
stroking Raven's neck, "but I'm not such a perfect warrior."
Rose flushed and dropped her gaze. "I've fallen off twice."

White Bear nodded again. "All young warriors have
trouble at first."

Rose stopped Raven at the gate to the track, stuck
her bare foot in the stirrup, and mounted. Gathering her
reins, she clucked to Swift Raven. They trotted once
around the track to warm up. Then she halted him next
to White Bear, who stood tall and proud by the railing in
front of the grandstand.

Biting her lip, Rose sat quiet in the saddle, waiting for him to speak.

Finally White Bear said in his deep voice, "A Sioux mounted on a fast-moving pony does not look down. She knows that the earth rushing by will make her head spin. To keep from falling, a warrior must always keep her eye on the enemy." The chief gave Rose such a grave look that goose bumps tingled up her spine.

Rose sat straighter. White Bear had said *she* and *her.* He wasn't just talking about Sioux warriors and riding.

"What if you don't know who the enemy is?" she asked.

"You will know." White Bear slapped Swift Raven on the rump, and the pony trotted off.

Blowing out a frustrated breath, Rose squeezed Raven into a lope. White Bear talked as if she were supposed to know who the enemy was. Was the chief referring to General Judson, who was an enemy of all Indians?

Except right now Rose didn't care about Judson the war hawk and his support of the Dawes Allotment Act. She only cared about Zane.

White Bear was right about one thing, though. The last time she'd practiced the Warrior Mount, she had looked at the ground, gotten dizzy, and taken a hard tumble. *Keep your eye on the enemy.* White Bear was telling her not to look down.

Rose caught her breath. Maybe the chief was also telling her that *he* knew who shot General Judson! The Sioux

moved like silent ghosts around the camp, seeing everything. But if White Bear knew who shot Judson, then why
wouldn't he tell her?

*The Sioux are too smart to get mixed up with white men's
problems,* she recalled Zane telling Mama. *They don't trust
us. And no wonder. An Indian expects a man to keep his word.
But we continue to break our promises.*

"Oh, fiddle," Rose muttered. It was all too confusing
and hard to figure. At this rate, she'd never be able to help
Mama free Zane. And now she needed to pay attention to
her riding or she'd take a tumble right at White Bear's feet.

Rose steered Raven down the straightaway in front of
the grandstand. When the pony was cantering smoothly in
a straight line, she took a deep breath. Dropping the short
reins on the pony's neck, she threw her right leg over the
saddle horn to the pony's left side. She grasped the horn
with both hands, kicked her left foot free of the stirrup too,
and slid forward toward Raven's shoulder.

Ready, go! Holding tight to the saddle horn, she tucked
her legs and dropped. Her bare feet hit the ground at a
run beside Raven's pounding hooves. *Don't look down!*
Eyes forward, she sprang up with the motion of her pony.
Still gripping the saddle horn, she threw her right leg over
the saddle, slid both feet into the stirrups, and pushed
herself to a sitting position.

I did it! Rose laughed aloud. *I did the Warrior Mount!*
At least this was *one* way she could help Mama. This trick

would surely convince Mr. Frontier to put her act in the show. She'd be such a success that he would *have* to keep them on with the Wild West.

Exhilarated, Rose turned Raven back toward White Bear. She was eager to thank him for his advice, and she hoped that she might still learn something from him that would help Zane. Only the chief was gone. She slowed Raven to a trot and glanced up and down the track, but he'd vanished.

Rose rapped her saddle horn with her fist. Would *no* one help her and Mama?

She practiced a few more tricks, but her mind kept wandering as she imagined Zane alone and miserable in the jail cell. *He must think we've abandoned him.* Rose tightened her fingers on the reins. *I won't abandon you, Zane. I'll figure out who shot General Judson.*

By the time she finished practicing, the racetrack crew had started raking the infield grass, readying the grounds for tonight's show. Rose slowed Raven to a walk for the final lap around the track, cooling him down. As he ambled clockwise toward the grandstand, Rose eyed the tiers of seats. She pictured the stagecoach careening around the backstretch turn. Shots from the bandits' pistols had rung out as the stage headed toward the grandstand.

Rose leaned over the pommel. "What do you think, Raven? Did General Judson's shooter fire then, too, hoping the bandits' shots would mask his?"

At the homestretch turn, Rose halted Raven and scanned the area around the grandstand. Her eyes narrowed as she picked out the porter's lodge, a small white clapboard building just beyond the steward's tower. A supply wagon was parked by the lodge. That had to be the wagon where the police had found Zane's revolver.

Questions filled Rose's head. Had the shooter stolen Zane's Colt from the tent, then run around the outside of the track to the right of the grandstand? Where had he stood when he fired the shot? *Near the wagon? Was that why he'd hidden the revolver there afterward?*

Rose glanced over her shoulder toward the campground. The tops of the tents were silhouetted against the western sky on the side of the track opposite the grandstand. If she was right, the shooter *had* to have known exactly where Zane's Colts were stashed. There had been scant time between Zane's act and the bandits' holdup to steal the revolver and get into position to hit the stagecoach.

Rose grimaced. Of course, she'd made the whole thing easier by leaving the gun box in plain sight on the sewing machine. Still, she and Mama had been right. The shooter had to be with the Wild West show. He had to know the layout of the camp and the timing of the acts.

Rose's skin crawled at the idea that a friend might have betrayed her family.

"My mind's awhirl with questions, Raven," Rose said as she steered the pony from the track. "I can't even remember multiplication. How will I figure all this out in time to help Zane?"

Dismounting outside the gate, Rose loosened the pony's cinch, then led him toward the barn. Comanche's head hung over the stall door. Rose wondered if the stallion was waiting for Zane.

Rose unlatched Raven's stall door. As she led him in, something glittery caught her eye. Frowning, she halted Raven to look more closely. A gold chain hung over the lip of the pony's empty feed bin. She reached out and picked up the chain. Dangling from one end was Pearson's pocket watch. Rose recognized the scrolled *WP* on the gold cover.

That's odd, Rose thought. The watch hadn't been there earlier when she'd tacked up Raven.

She slipped the chain through her fingers. The clasp was broken. Had Pearson lost the watch? If so, who had put it in Swift Raven's stall? *White Bear?* Had the chief left it for her to find? Was he trying to tell her something about Pearson?

What if you don't know who the enemy is? she'd asked him. *You will know.*

Prickles ran up Rose's spine. Was White Bear telling her what she already suspected—that the shooter was someone she knew? *Pearson?*

Rose scratched her head. That didn't make sense. Mr. Pearson had been in the steward's tower, announcing the show. He wouldn't have had time to get Zane's Colt from the tent.

A strained, reedy noise interrupted Rose's thoughts. She glanced out the stall door. Oliver strode into view, his cheeks puffed as he tried to whistle a tune. Rose vaguely recognized "Oh! Susanna."

Rose slid the watch and chain into her pocket. William Pearson had been with the show since it began. He was Mr. Frontier's partner and friend. Even Oliver would think she was crazy if she accused the man of being involved in General Judson's shooting just because she'd found his watch.

Rose peered over the top of the stall door. "Did you swallow an ailing songbird?" she asked.

Neck reddening, Oliver stopped in his tracks. "I didn't know anyone was here." He held up a book, *The Adventures of Huckleberry Finn,* then pointed to some sycamore trees beyond the buffalo corral. "I was headed to that shady grove to read. Your mama says you need to catch up on your studies, too."

Stepping closer, he glanced hesitantly into the stall. When Raven ambled over, Oliver reached out one hand and gingerly touched the pony's nose.

Rose unbuckled the throat strap on the bridle. "Aren't you going to be in the show tonight?" she asked as she slipped the bridle over Raven's ears.

Oliver shook his head. "Mr. Frontier's invited a host of bigwigs to ride in the stagecoach for the grand parade. Something about public relations. I heard him talking to Mr. Pearson." When Raven began to snuffle Oliver's cheek, he stiffened. "Mr. Frontier said there wouldn't be room for you in the coach, either," he added between clenched teeth. Suddenly, he let out a bark of laughter and pushed Raven away. "That tickles!"

Rose almost dropped the bridle. "Mr. Frontier doesn't want me in the coach?" she repeated. Then she shrugged, pretending she didn't care. "Well, that's fine with me," she said quickly, though a chill swept through her. Were Mama's words coming true? Did Mr. Frontier no longer want them with the show?

She took off Raven's saddle, trying to act unruffled. "What about 'Raid on the Homesteaders' Cabin'? Will he need us for that?"

"He didn't say."

Rose swung open the door, and Oliver stepped back as she carried out the saddle. "I'll bet he and Mr. Pearson didn't say anything about Zane rotting in jail, either," she added bitterly as she set the saddle against the wall.

Oliver dropped his gaze to the book in his hands.

Rose snorted. "I thought so. I believe they're *glad* he was arrested so the precious show can go on."

"They argued again," Oliver said quietly. "Mr. Pearson said the show is sixty thousand dollars in debt."

Rose's mouth fell open. "That's a powerful lot of money. No wonder they're worried about the show closing."

"Pearson is only worried about his share of the money,"

Oliver confided. "He's made it plain to Mr. Frontier that he wants to quit the Wild West."

Rose chewed on a fingernail. Pearson again. The man's name kept pricking her like a thorn. She stepped back into the stall and rubbed Raven's sweaty back with a feed sack, then threw a rope over his neck and led him to a corral full of mules. When she turned him out, he trotted into the middle of the long-eared animals and started grazing on the sparse grass.

"Oliver, I've got a storm of questions whirling in my brain," Rose confided as they walked back to the barn. "And it seems like I gotta answer them if I'm to help Zane."

Oliver nodded. "That's the way I feel about inventions. Like I've got to read everything about them before—"

Suddenly she grabbed his hand. "Come on. I need your help."

He planted his legs like a balky mule. "What about *The Adventures of Huckleberry Finn?* I'm supposed to be doing my reading lesson now."

Rose tugged on his arm. "Oliver, I'm asking you to be in a real adventure, not one written on pages."

He hesitated only a moment, then dropped the book by the stall door and came with her. "Where are we going?" he asked as they hurried from the stable yard.

"To figure out where the shooter was hiding." She glanced at him over her shoulder, realizing that she was still holding his hand. Blushing, she let go of it.

"The sh-shooter?" Oliver stuttered. His step slowed.

"What's wrong?" Rose asked. "Scared he's lying in wait for us?"

Sticking his thumbs in his suspenders, Oliver faked a swagger. "Naw."

Rose grinned to herself as they passed the ticket wagon and went through the main entrance to the grandstand. Ignoring the stairs to the tiers of seats, she hurried along the front of the grandstand where the audience could watch the show from behind the railing.

"Where are we going?" Oliver asked, whispering even though there was no one else around.

"To the porter's lodge," Rose whispered back.

When they reached the far end of the grandstand, Rose halted. In front of her was the steward's tower, its wooden steps zigzagging up to the platform. Just beyond was the clapboard porter's lodge, with a flatbed wagon parked in front. Rose pointed to the wagon. "That's where they found Zane's revolver."

Oliver pushed back his hat. "Golly, this *is* an adventure."

"The Colt was hidden under a canvas tarp," Rose said as they walked over to the wagon. "Anyone could have put it there after General Judson was shot."

Grabbing the rim of the front wheel, Rose used the spokes like ladder rungs to climb into the seat. Then she sat and faced the track.

"If the shooter sat here, he *did* have a clear view," she

said excitedly as Oliver climbed up beside her. "I'll bet he took the revolver from our tent and ran around the outside of the track." She circled counterclockwise with her arm. "If he ran behind the supply tent"—she pointed to the peaked roof on her left—"no one would've seen him. Then he jumped onto this wagon, just like we did, and waited for the stagecoach to come onto the track. It's the perfect spot."

Oliver nodded intently as if watching the scene unfold.

Raising one arm, Rose pretended to aim a pistol. "I can picture it now. The stagecoach is rounding the homestretch turn." She squinted one eye and looked down the pretend barrel. "The shot would be tricky, but a marksman could do it. As the stage heads down the straightaway, he sights in General Judson, who's sitting . . ." Rose's voice trailed off, and slowly she lowered her hand.

"Who's sitting . . ." Oliver urged.

Rose turned toward him. "I was going to say 'who's sitting by the window,'" she said, suddenly breathless. "Only *Senator North* was by the window. I was in the middle. General Judson was on the far side of the stagecoach."

"The shooter *was* an excellent marksman."

"Not just excellent. *Uncanny.* Unless—" Rose's mind raced. Her mouth went dry. "Oliver, I don't believe the shooter was trying to hit General Judson. He was aiming for Senator North!"

CHAPTER 12

DETERMINATION

Oliver blinked. "You mean the shooter missed Senator North and hit General Judson by mistake?"

Rose nodded. "It had to be! Not even a sharpshooter as fine as Zane could hit General Judson on the far side of the stagecoach."

She pictured the bullet lodged in the back of the stagecoach. *A little lower and it might have been your ear shot off,* Zane had told her jokingly. Perhaps he'd been more right than he knew.

"And if the shooter was trying to hit *Senator North* and missed, that's double proof the person wasn't Zane," Rose went on. "He'd *never* miss a target that easy."

Oliver took off his straw hat and scratched his head. "I don't know, Rose. Why would someone shoot at Senator North? Whereas Mr. Pearson said a lot of people wanted to put a bullet in General Judson."

Sighing, Rose slouched on the wagon seat. "You're right.

It's like my good ideas don't make sense once I speak them."

While she pondered the problem, several *vaqueros* trotted onto the track, warming up their ponies. For the show, Mr. Frontier made them dress in wide-brimmed sombreros and fancy embroidered bolero jackets gleaming with silver buttons and braid, although they wore denim pants and cotton shirts around camp.

"Come on." Rose stood up. "It's suppertime. We need to eat, and I should see if Mama needs help before the show."

They jumped down from the wagon. As they passed behind the steward's tower, Rose tilted her head and looked up at the roofed platform high above. From there, the announcer could see the entire racetrack.

Rose glanced back at the wagon. "Oliver, if the shooter was in the wagon, why didn't Mr. Pearson see him?"

"Who knows? He was probably watching the stagecoach and bandits like everybody else, Rose. It was very dramatic."

Except Mr. Pearson had seen the act hundreds of times before. Rose slid her hand into her pocket and let the chain flow through her fingers. Had Pearson seen the shooter? Is that what White Bear was telling her? If so, why did Pearson let the police arrest Zane?

"All this wondering is turning my brain into Cook's mush," Rose admitted as they set off again. "I wish I could make sense of it all. One thing's true for sure, though—Mr. Pearson's name keeps coming to the tip of my tongue."

Oliver cleared his throat. "Mine, too."

Rose glanced sharply at him. "You know something else, Oliver?"

"Well, I don't know how this figures in, but when we came back from town today I typed a letter for Mr. Pearson. It was to a Senator Dawes in Massachusetts. Pearson told the senator that he supported the Dawes Allotment Act. He said that while General Judson was recuperating, the bill should not lose steam."

"Why is Pearson so interested in the Dawes Allotment Act?" Rose asked. "I saw an article about it on his desk the day I was snooping."

"I don't know." Oliver shrugged. "I do know one thing, though." He threw back his shoulders and declared, "The bill is wrong. Mr. Frontier says if it's made into a law, the Indians will be left with nothing. Congress needs to vote it down."

"Oliver, I do believe you'll grow up to be president." Rose rubbed her forehead, trying to figure how the odious Dawes Act fit in with the shooting.

White Bear might know. The Sioux chief kept his nose out of white men's politics, yet he knew everything that affected his tribe. Rose suspected he could help her make sense of the puzzle. However, his vanishing act also suggested he was wary of getting tangled in the investigation.

"Let's speak about this at dinner," Rose told Oliver. "Cook's frying chicken, and the *vaqueros* are reminding me that there's a show tonight."

Oliver agreed and the two hurried to the mess tent, the smell of sizzling chicken making their mouths water. As they neared the tent, Mr. Frontier strode up.

"Oliver, I need to speak to Miss Rose." He dismissed his son with a toss of his hand, as if he were shooing away flies.

Oliver hesitated. Then he mumbled, "Yes, sir," and slunk into the tent.

"So, Rose, you'll be my settlers' daughter tonight?" Mr. Frontier asked. Although his tone was jovial, he had dark rings around his eyes and his mustache was ragged. "No bonnets catching on fire? We've got to impress our audience if we want the show to go on."

Rose looked sideways at him. Perhaps he truly was caught up in worries about the show. That didn't mean she'd forgive him for forgetting about Zane.

"Yes, sir," she said. "I'll do it right. And, sir?" She mustered up her courage. This was her chance to plug her act and help ease Mama's fears about being dismissed from the troupe. "I wanted to talk to you about riding in the show."

Mr. Frontier crooked one brow.

Rose took it as encouragement. "I've been practicing my trick riding. I can do the Warrior Stand, the Warrior Mount, and the Dead Man's Drag. And Raven can rear, bow, and walk on his hind legs. While Zane's in jail, I can take his place in the show."

Mr. Frontier smiled and patted her arm as if she were a babe. "That's an interesting offer, Rose, but no audience wants to watch a girl ride astride a horse. They'd think it's, well, *indecent.* Besides, this is the Wild West show. Folks want soldiers, buffalo hunters, and Indians, not little ladies. And we aim to please the paying audience," he added with a sigh, giving her arm another pat before walking away.

Bile filled Rose's throat, and if she hadn't been such a *little lady,* she would have used it to shine Mr. Frontier's boots. He hadn't even asked to see her tricks! He hadn't even offered her a chance!

Furious, she bustled into the mess tent and pushed her way into the serving line. She knew her trick-riding act was as good as any of the others.

Rose grabbed a plate and held it out. Cook piled a mountain of mashed potatoes, fatback beans, chicken, and corn pone onto it. Rose hunted among the diners for Mama, who was nowhere to be found.

Rose's heart felt as heavy as her plate. Not only was she failing Zane, she was failing Mama. If she were a boy, she knew Mr. Frontier would have let her ride in the show.

As Rose walked past the long wooden tables, she took in the cowboys, soldiers, roustabouts, and *vaqueros* shoveling food into their mouths. Did they have any idea the show was sixty thousand dollars in debt? Where would they go if it folded? Where would she and Mama go?

Then she thought about the Sioux and the other Indians in the troupe. Many relied on the show for money to send home to their families. If the Dawes Act took away their lands, and Mr. Frontier no longer could pay them for performing, what would they have left?

The idea made *her* want to shoot General Judson — which made her think that her hunch about Senator North didn't make sense after all.

Life was just too ornery. Sighing deeply, Rose made her way to Oliver's table. She set her plate across from him and slid onto the bench alongside Billy Dees. He was intently mopping up gravy with a slice of bread.

"You missed a lick," she teased halfheartedly.

Billy Dees waved the bread at her. Gravy dripped from his mustache. "You plannin' on anything excitin' fer tonight's show, Miss Rose?" he asked.

She shook her head. "Mr. Frontier won't hear of a *lady* riding in the show."

At the word *lady,* Oliver let out a bark of laughter.

"Too bad," Billy Dees said. "I've seen you practice, and your trick riding is a pleasure to behold. How 'bout another shootin' fer excitement, then? I hear Frontier's got the stagecoach bursting with generals and senators. Anyone going to faint in your lap tonight during the Dry Gulch holdup?"

"No shootings, Billy Dees. Remember? The police got the culprit locked in jail."

"Culprit, my foot." Billy Dees snorted. "Zane's a great shot as long as his target don't breathe. I 'member when I took the boy huntin'. He dang near wet his britches when I told him to shoot a rabbit."

"Why didn't you tell that to Police Chief Whallen?" Rose asked. "Zane needs all the help he can get to prove he's innocent. Since he's been in jail, seems like his friends have quit him."

Billy Dees banged his spoon on the table. "We did no such thing," he sputtered. "Pop Whittaker and me went to see Zane right after you and your mama visited him. Only that puffed-up jailer wouldn't let us in."

Billy helped himself to a drumstick from her plate. "Pop and me even went to see that self-important windbag who calls himself a police chief. Wouldn't even listen to us. Told us the evidence was strong enough to send Zane to jail for ten years."

Ten years! Suddenly, the smell of the chicken and beans made Rose's stomach churn. She pushed away her plate.

"Rose, you all right?" Oliver asked.

"I'm not as hungry as I thought." Swinging around on the bench, she stood up. "See you tonight at the show," she told them before hurrying from the mess tent.

When she reached her own tent, she was dismayed to see that Mama wasn't there either. *Where is she?* Rose grumbled. She needed to talk to Mama about all the thoughts spinning in her head like spokes on a wheel.

Feeling sorrowful, Rose went to the corner to change from her dusty clothes. Propped on her pillow was her school slate with a note from Mama written in chalk: "Gone to help Alma. Baby's arriving."

Rose smiled as she sank onto the cot. Mama had a pile of troubles, yet it didn't stop her from helping others.

And I can't even help Zane! Rose felt the hot flush of rising tears. She jumped from the cot and took off her dress and pinafore. Then she yanked her hair back in a ribbon and poured water from the pitcher into the washbasin. Crying wasn't going to solve Zane's problems, she told herself as she splashed her face and neck. Clear thinking would.

And clear thinking told her that somehow Mr. Pearson and the Dawes Act were mighty involved in the shooting. She just wasn't sure how.

Rose dried her face, realizing again that she had to see White Bear. She pulled on her calico settler's dress, grabbed her bonnet, and tied it loosely around her neck. Then she raced from the tent. Since she wasn't helping Zane or riding in the grand parade, she had plenty of time to talk to the chief before "Raid on the Homesteaders' Cabin."

First she needed to check on Mama. Rose hadn't seen Mama since they'd returned, downhearted, from their trip into town to talk to Abigail Reed. Perhaps Mama had good news about Zane. Then Rose could quit worrying.

The Nelsons' tent was two down. Calvin Nelson was a trumpet player in the band. Alma was his wife of a year. It was Alma's first baby, and Rose knew she was anxious.

When she reached the tent, she heard Mama's soothing voice and Alma's exhausted one. Rose was about to call into the tent when a scream made her hair rise.

If having babies made you scream like that, Rose wasn't at all interested.

"Mama?" she whispered into the tent when it was quiet.

"Come in, Rose, but be quick."

Rose sidled into the tent. In the far corner, Alma rested on her cot. She was covered with a quilt. Her face was flushed, her eyes were closed, and she panted as if she'd just run a race.

Rose had seen foals and calves born, plopping out all wet and long-legged, the mares and cows unconcerned by the whole affair. She knew birthing a baby was not such an easy matter.

"What is it, Rose?" Mama wrung out a rag and placed it on Alma's forehead.

"I thought maybe you had news about Zane."

Mama shook her head. "Nothing. I've been with Alma since noon."

Rose opened her mouth, ready to tell Mama about the gold chain and her hunch that the shooter might have been gunning for Senator North. But then Alma whimpered in pain, and Mama leaned forward to whisper soothing words.

"Would you or Alma like tea?" Rose asked instead.

Mama smiled. "Two cups of tea would be wonderful. Thank you. Are you ready for the show?"

"Yes, ma'am. I'm just being the settlers' daughter tonight." Alma's face began to twist into another scream, and Rose made a hasty exit, Alma's wail following her.

When she reached the quiet of her own tent, she lit the spirit lamp, which they used to heat water.

She filled the kettle with water and set it over the lamp's flame. While the water heated, Rose thought about life after Papa had died. Zane was seventeen then and had jumped right into his father's shoes, taking over the sharpshooting act. At first he'd missed more targets than he hit. Soon, however, his flamboyant ways and daring shooting had made him the talk of every show.

A lump formed in Rose's throat. What would life be without Zane? She'd already lost Papa. She couldn't stand to lose Zane, too.

Wheeee. The kettle began to sing. Rose blew out the lamp, then carefully poured two mugs of steaming water. When the tea was brewed, she carried the mugs to Alma's tent. It was quiet. Perhaps now Mama would have a few minutes to speak of Zane.

Rose peered inside. Mama was asleep, her body limp in the rocker. Alma appeared asleep, too. Her face was sweaty and slack with exhaustion, but there was no sign of a babe. Rose tiptoed in, set the mugs on Alma's bedside table, and quietly left without speaking. Mama had enough problems.

Outside the tent, Rose tied on her bonnet. Squaring her shoulders, she marched in the direction of the Sioux camp.

It was time she stopped relying on Mama. It was time she stepped into Zane's boots.

It was time she talked to White Bear.

CHAPTER 13
A TELLTALE SILENCE

The campground was teeming with tour groups, and farther off Rose could see lines snaking from the ticket booth to the grandstand. In the Sioux camp, Mr. Frontier led a cluster of journalists and curiosity seekers among the tipis. When Rose reached White Bear's tipi, she saw that White Bear's sons, One Feather and Thunder Cloud, sat out front, whittling sticks with their knives, their stern expressions keeping anyone from getting too close. When One Feather saw her, he jutted his head toward the tipi, motioning for her to go inside. Was the chief expecting her? Rose took a deep breath, then slowly drew back the buffalo-skin flap. White Bear was alone.

Eyes lowered respectfully, Rose slipped into the tipi and settled cross-legged next to White Bear. She took off her bonnet and set it in her lap. Tipping her chin, she stared silently ahead, waiting until White Bear was ready to speak.

In the distance, Rose heard the Cowboy Band play "Camptown Races" and "My Old Kentucky Home." Then she heard Mr. Pearson announce the grand parade. As each act entered the racetrack, the crowd gave the performers a rousing welcome.

It seemed like hours before White Bear finally broke the silence.

"Rose would make a good warrior," he said, a hint of amusement in his voice. "Now that she can ride like a Sioux."

Rose sat taller. "Never as good as White Bear, Chief of the Dakota Sioux. He's such a brave, wise warrior, he knows *everything*."

White Bear made a noise in his throat as if he agreed with the slightly overblown praise. Rose rushed on, wanting to ask a bushel of questions before the chief dismissed her.

"Which is why I come to White Bear and humbly request his help. *Humbly*," she repeated.

The chief's eyes crinkled with laughter. "Tell me your troubles."

"Not just my troubles, Ma-to-sea. Troubles for your people, too. General Judson and men like him are trying to get a law passed called the Dawes Allotment Act. It would take away Indian land and give it to white men."

"White men already take our land."

"They would be able to take your reservation, too. The Sioux would be forced to live on smaller parcels. The rest would be sold to white men."

White Bear's jaw tightened. "Another promise you do not keep."

"Not me!" Rose said hastily. "And not Zane, or Senator North. And there are other white people who do not want this law."

"General Judson and Mr. Pearson, they like this law."

Rose glanced over at him. "How did you know about Mr. Pearson?"

White Bear only crossed his arms.

"I know you left me his watch and chain. Where did you find it? What were you trying to tell me? Did Pearson see the person who shot General Judson?"

White Bear arched one brow.

Does that mean yes or no? Frustrated, Rose twirled the bonnet ties in her hand.

She started over. "Chief White Bear, this is where I need your help. I know you don't meddle in white men's problems. And I don't blame you. We certainly deserve to stew in our own miseries. Except for Zane. He *didn't* shoot General Judson."

"Your brother does not have a warrior's heart."

"That's the same thing Billy Dees said. So if Zane's innocent, someone else is guilty. But who? My innards tell me that somehow the Dawes Act and Mr. Pearson have something to do with Judson being shot."

"Your instincts are wise."

"If that's true, then I need to think on Pearson."

Holding up her hand, she counted as she talked. "One, I know he wants to sell his share of the Wild West. Two, he wants to buy land in South Dakota. Three, he—"

Rose inhaled so abruptly that she made a strangling noise. "That's it! He wants to buy land in South Dakota! 'Dirt cheap,'" she repeated Oliver's words. "No wonder he supports the Dawes Act. If the law goes through, he can buy reservation land for a song!"

White Bear nodded.

"You knew all this?"

"White Bear knows many things."

Rose groaned. "Except I still don't know what this has to do with Zane. Mr. Pearson wouldn't have shot General Judson. They're allies."

Suddenly her eyes widened and she clapped her hand to her mouth. "Unless I was right," she breathed through her fingers. "Senator North was the target. *Not* Judson."

She looked sideways at the chief, but he only waited.

"No." She shook her head wildly. "That doesn't make sense." She uncrossed her legs and rubbed her foot, which had gone plumb to sleep. "Pearson might have *wanted* to shoot Senator North. The senator was working hard to make sure the bill wouldn't pass. But Pearson *couldn't* have run to the tent and retrieved Zane's Colt. He was announcing the show."

"Sioux also hear many things."

"What do you mean? You heard something important?"

The chief stared stonily ahead.

"Why won't you tell me?" Her voice rose with frustration. *Stop chattering like a squirrel!* she heard Mama scold. Rose pressed her lips together before more words spilled out.

"The Sioux keep a coyote's distance from white men's problems," White Bear said. "Rose needs to solve her problems." Closing his eyes, he bowed his head and slowed his breathing as if listening to something within himself.

White Bear was saying it was up to her. Rose closed her own eyes, squeezing them tight so she wouldn't be tempted to peek. She could hear White Bear's steady breathing. She could hear the crowds outside the tents and the audience in the grandstand. She could hear Mr. Pearson announcing Billy Dees's broncobusting act.

"For the night creatures, it is the silence that signals the enemy," White Bear said in a voice that seemed to swirl around her like a breeze. "When the night sounds are quiet, the animals know an enemy is near. Listen, Rose, and you will know the enemy."

Rose pressed her fingers against her eyes. *Silence signals the enemy. When the night sounds are quiet.* Was White Bear talking about the night Judson was shot?

She let her mind drift back to that night. After she had put Zane's revolvers in the tent, she'd hurried to board the stagecoach. Billy Dees had finished riding Old Lightning. Pop Whittaker had hollered, "Time for the Dry Gulch Stage."

She thought about the sounds she'd heard that night: Pop Whittaker's voice. The crack of the whip. The creak of the stage as it rolled onto the track. The pounding of the horses' hooves.

Rose caught her breath. The silence! Now she knew what White Bear meant. She knew what sounds were missing that night. Mr. Pearson hadn't announced "Attack on the Dry Gulch Stage"!

Opening her eyes, Rose touched White Bear's arm. "Now I understand what you mean by 'listen for the silence.' And I know why you left Mr. Pearson's watch for me to find. Because *he* shot General Judson!"

White Bear nodded with satisfaction.

"I told myself he didn't have time to run and get Zane's revolver because he was in the tower announcing 'Attack on the Dry Gulch Stage,'" Rose rushed on. "But he wasn't in the tower! He didn't make the announcement because he was hurrying to the tent to get Zane's revolver. Then he ran back and climbed onto the wagon where he'd have a clear shot at the stagecoach. He aimed at Senator North. He wanted to kill Senator North to keep him from campaigning against the Dawes Act. *Only he shot General Judson by mistake.*"

Rose was so excited, she jumped to her feet. White Bear sat quietly as she paced in front of him.

"That's why he never hired a lawyer to help Zane," she said bitterly. "He *wanted* the police to believe Zane was the shooter. Then they wouldn't look for anyone else."

White Bear touched his finger to his lips. Rose cocked her head and listened.

"Tonight the Wild West is host to a stagecoach full of Louisville's finest citizens," she heard Mr. Pearson announce. "Mayor and Mrs. Reed, Senator Samuel North—"

Rose's brows shot up. Senator North was a passenger on the stage! What if Pearson tried again to shoot him? This time, he might be successful.

"Thank you, White Bear." Without thinking, she gave the chief a hug around the shoulders. "Now I must hurry and warn Senator North," she added as she dashed from the tipi.

Rose sped toward the track entrance, where the team of horses waited to pull the stagecoach onto the track. Pop Whittaker was in the driver's seat. The stagecoach doors were shut. Through the window, Rose could see Senator North sitting on the right side, in the same place he'd been before. That meant he'd be a perfect target for Pearson.

She hollered, "Pop! Wait!" but her words were lost in the din of the crowd. By the time she reached the entrance, the stagecoach would be racing onto the track. Rose held her breath as she ran, listening for Mr. Pearson's voice announcing the act, but the steward's tower was silent.

Her heart took a tumble. *Pearson was setting himself up for the shot!*

"Pop!" She waved her arm, but Pop Whittaker cracked the whip and the stagecoach rumbled through the gate onto the track. The bandits rode up to the entrance, waiting for their cue to chase the stage. Behind them the cavalry waited on their mounts.

Rose slowed. She knew her suspicions would sound like ramblings. Would anyone believe her?

She wound her way through the cavalry horses and ran up to Mr. Frontier. He was mounted on Ranger, ready to ride to the rescue. "Sir! It's Mr. Pearson—"

Mr. Frontier didn't even look down at her. All his attention was on his mount, who was attempting to rear. "Another time, Rose."

"But, sir—"

"Whoa," Mr. Frontier commanded, but Ranger swished his tail and danced sideways, almost knocking Rose over. Over the outside fence, she spotted the stagecoach heading for the backstretch turn. Time was running out!

Rose spied Con Hardy, who'd gotten off his cow pony, Belle, to check the cinch, and in a flash, she knew what she had to do.

Racing up behind Belle, Rose planted two hands on the pony's rump and propelled herself up and onto the saddle. The mare skittered forward, yanking the reins from Con's hand.

Reaching down, Rose snatched the reins and dug her heels into Belle's sides. "Hiya!" she called, and the mare tore through the entrance gate and onto the track.

Rose hunkered down on Belle's neck. They flew up the backstretch just as the stagecoach swung into the turn.

She had to make it in time to warn Senator North!

The stagecoach was flying, but it was no match for a lone rider on a galloping pony. Rose caught up to the coach's right side as it headed toward the steward's tower. She glanced ahead, trying to glimpse the wagon in front of the porter's lodge. There! A man stood on the seat, partially hidden in the shadows of the grandstand. His arm was raised as if he was aiming a pistol in the direction of the track.

Rose's heart leaped. She steered Belle closer to the whirling wheels. Behind her she could hear the bandits shooting at the stagecoach. Any minute, the coach would be within pistol range of Pearson.

Belle drew forward next to the stagecoach door. When Mrs. Reed saw Rose, she clutched her heart and shrieked. Senator North peered out the side window, his expression incredulous.

"Senator North!" Rose screamed. "You're in trouble! Get down!"

Rose heard the report of a gun to her right. Pearson!

Galloping next to the stagecoach, she was a perfect target.

You must escape from your enemy. Rose threw her right leg over to the left side of the saddle. Holding onto the saddle horn, she started to drop beside Belle's left side when she heard a second crack.

A searing pain pierced her right shoulder.

Rose cried out but managed to hang on. Belle and the stagecoach flew past the wagon and the steward's tower. The bandits came roaring around the turn after the coach. Pop Whittaker was hollering, "Whoa, whoa," trying to slow the team.

Rose tugged on Belle's reins, and the pony dropped back behind the coach. Rose could feel warm blood seeping through her sleeve. The pain in her shoulder made her head swim.

Her arm weakened; her grip loosened on the saddle horn. She couldn't hold on.

Pulling on the left rein, Rose steered Belle toward the inside of the track and away from the bandits' horses, which thundered toward her. As she slipped to the ground, she pushed off Belle's side, hoping to escape the pony's churning hooves. She hit the dirt and tumbled onto her injured shoulder.

Everything went black.

CHAPTER 14
WELCOME SURPRISES

The pain brought Rose back to consciousness. She grabbed her shoulder, and her fingers came away sticky with blood. Dust swirled around her as the bandits raced past. Rising on her good arm, she spotted the stagecoach, which had halted in front of the grandstand. Was the senator all right?

Mr. Frontier galloped up, slid Ranger to a halt, and leaped off his horse. "What in tarnation, Rose? There are less dangerous ways to get me to watch your trick riding!"

"It was Mr. Pearson, sir! He was trying to shoot Senator North!" She nodded her head toward the wagon, but Mr. Frontier's gaze was on her.

"You're hurt!" His face blanched under his Stetson, and he dropped to one knee. "Hold still. You must've injured your shoulder in the fall." He pulled off his neckerchief.

"No, Mr. Pearson *shot* me!" Rose struggled to rise. Would no one listen to her? "You've got to catch him.

He was on the wagon by the porter's lodge. He was trying to shoot Senator North. You've got to make sure Senator North is all right."

"Pearson?" Mr. Frontier tossed a glance over his shoulder, then stood up. "There's no one by the wagon. And here comes Senator North, right as rain."

Rose glanced to her left as Senator North strode around the back of the stagecoach. The bandits had leaped back onto their horses. The cavalry was pursuing them around the track. Rose exhaled with relief, glad to see that the senator was all right.

"Mr. Frontier," Senator North called as he hustled toward them. "There was a man with a pistol standing on that wagon. He was shooting—" He cut his sentence short when he saw Rose. "Are you all right? I didn't realize anyone had been hurt."

"It was Mr. Pearson with the pistol, Senator North," Rose said. "He shot me when I was riding beside the stagecoach. You've got to go after him. Don't let him get away—"

"Pearson can wait." Kneeling, Mr. Frontier began wrapping her shoulder with his neckerchief. "You're losing a lot of blood."

"All this time we thought the target was General Judson," Rose rushed on. She had to make them understand that the shooter was Pearson, not Zane. "But Mr. Pearson was gunning for you, Senator."

"Me?" The senator's mouth tightened. "Are you sure?"

"Yes. Pearson wants to buy reservation land in South Dakota," Rose explained. "Ouch!" She jerked her arm away when Mr. Frontier tightened the bandage. "That hurts."

The senator crouched beside her. "Rose, what does that have to do with Pearson shooting at me?"

"He wants the Dawes Act to get passed. He doesn't want you opposing it. That's why he shot at you. This time he missed and shot me. Last time he missed and shot General Judson." Rose grew lightheaded. "That's how I knew it wasn't Zane. My brother *never* misses."

Taking out a white handkerchief, Senator North gently dabbed at Rose's forehead. "Then thank you for saving my life, Miss Taylor," he said solemnly. "Now rest easy. You're looking a mite pale."

"I feel a mite pale." Rose's lips could barely form words. Her skin felt clammy, but she had to make sure the senator understood about Zane. "Senator North." She squeezed his arm. "Promise me you'll get my brother out of jail."

"I promise."

"Thank you." Rose's eyelids felt heavy and drifted shut.

"Put her in the stagecoach and get her to a doctor," she heard Senator North say. She felt a strong arm under her back and one behind her knees, and someone lifted her high. Then a roar filled her head, so loud that Rose forced her eyes open. She shook her head, wondering if a bee was buzzing inside her brain, but then she realized it was the audience.

"They're calling for you, Rose," Senator North said as he strode beside Mr. Frontier, who was carrying her to the stagecoach.

"Me?" Rose murmured. Taking a deep breath, she mustered her strength and lifted her head to look. The audience was on its feet. Ladies flapped their handkerchiefs and men waved their hats.

"They're calling for the trick-riding gal," Mr. Frontier said, adding with a chuckle, "Danged if I wasn't wrong."

"They liked my riding?" Rose asked. Raising her good arm, she waved weakly toward the grandstand.

Senator North climbed into the coach and carefully took Rose from Mr. Frontier. Rose grimaced as the two men lifted her into the stagecoach.

Mrs. Reed was there. "Put her next to me," she said.

Rose lay on the seat and rested her head in Mrs. Reed's lap, trying to keep her shoulder from touching anything. She shivered, and Mrs. Reed covered her with a shawl.

"I need to take good care of you, Rose Taylor," the mayor's wife said. "I believe there's a surprise for you later tonight."

A surprise? Rose wanted to ask, but then Pop Whittaker slapped the reins, the team jerked the stagecoach forward, and a jolt of pain made her grit her teeth. As they headed from the track, the crowd was still cheering.

"They—they think it was . . . all . . . part of . . . the act," Rose haltingly told Senator North, who sat across from her.

He laughed. "They do, indeed, but I hope it's an act we will never repeat."

Licking her dry lips, she added, "Senator, I'm glad I warned you in time, but I'm sorry Mr. Pearson got away."

"I imagine the police will find him," Senator North said grimly. The team halted, and Mr. Frontier, who had followed the stagecoach on Ranger, flung open the door.

"Rose, some friends of yours would like to see you."

Rose frowned. Her head was foggy, her arm ached, chills raced up her spine, and her dress sleeve was bloody. She was hardly fit to receive friends.

Mr. Frontier stepped back. Senator North and Mrs. Reed helped Rose sit up so she could look out the stagecoach door. Pop Whittaker, Billy Dees, Mustang Jack, the bandits, and the cavalry were all gathered outside the coach. In front of them, White Bear, Thunder Cloud, One Feather, and Leaping Elk stood flanking a man.

Rose caught her breath. The man was Pearson! His head hung on his chest; his hands were tethered behind his back.

Without a word, White Bear handed Mr. Frontier a pistol. Then the chief bowed his head, and silently the four Sioux vanished through the crowd of performers.

"They caught him," Rose said. Then a wave of nausea swept through her and she slumped into Mrs. Reed's lap.

Rose groaned. Her eyes fluttered open. Where was she? Why did her shoulder hurt like fire?

She blinked in the dim light. Shadows from a kerosene lamp flickered over her head, and she realized that she was staring at the ceiling of their tent.

"Rose?" A face smiled down at her. Dark hair. Blue eyes. Could it be—?

"Zane!" Rose croaked.

"In the flesh." Her brother grinned.

Hot tears filled Rose's eyes. "What are you doing here? Why aren't you in jail?"

"Still Nosy Rose." Zane laughed. "I reckon that hard spill didn't hurt your head one bit."

"Oh, I'm so happy to see you!" Rose lifted her arms to hug him, but a sharp pain made her wince.

Mama leaned over the cot. "Stay quiet, Rose. Your shoulder has a flesh wound, and your ribs are bruised from the fall. The doctor said you'll be fine with rest."

"It was worth it. They caught Mr. Pearson!" Rose propped herself up on her good arm. "And Zane's free." She smiled happily at her brother, but then frowned in confusion. "How long have I been in bed?"

"Not long. It isn't even midnight yet," Mama said. "Alma had her baby and Mr. Frontier brought you here all about the same time."

"Then how'd Zane get out of jail so fast?"

"Abigail," Zane explained. "While you were riding to

Senator North's rescue, she came to mine. She threatened to starve herself if her papa wouldn't let her talk to Police Chief Whallen. Mayor Reed finally relented."

"So that's what Mrs. Reed meant by a surprise," Rose said.

Mama nodded. "I believe the mayor's wife had quite a bit to do with her husband's change of mind."

Rose fell back on her pillow. "I'm so glad they caught Mr. Pearson."

"Thanks to White Bear and the other Sioux men," Zane said. "Pearson was about to flee in a carriage he had waiting behind the porter's lodge. He didn't get very far."

Mama's eyes twinkled. "Guess what they found in the carriage? A suitcase filled with sixty thousand dollars. Mr. Pearson had been stealing from the show."

"No wonder the Wild West was losing money all this time," Rose said.

Senator North poked his head into the tent. "Any chance I can see the heroine of the show?"

Mama smiled down at Rose. "There's quite a line of people outside waiting to see you."

"I'm fine, Mama. Let them come in."

"One at a time," Mama cautioned.

Senator North strode into the tent and tipped his head. "Miss Rose, I do believe some color is back in your pretty cheeks."

She blushed.

"I just wanted to give you my regards before I head down to the police station. I aim to see that Mr. Pearson stays in jail for a long time."

Zane chuckled. "He'll love the fancy accommodations."

"I also wanted to see if there's anything I can do for you, Rose," he added. "To thank you for saving my life."

"Oh, there is." She struggled to sit up. "You need to go to Washington, D.C., and keep fighting against the Dawes Act," she declared passionately. "Those congressmen need to understand that Indians have rights, too. You need to tell the senators and representatives that they should treat the Indians with respect. And that we need to stop lying and breaking our promises."

Senator North looked impressed. "I couldn't have said it better, Miss Taylor."

"Perhaps you should take my sister to Washington with you," Zane teased. "She might make those war hawks take notice."

Everybody laughed except Rose, who tried to but winced instead. When Senator North left, Mr. Frontier and Oliver peered hesitantly into the tent. "Any chance I can see my fancy-riding gal?" Mr. Frontier asked.

Mama pursed her lips. "Are you sure you can handle more visitors, Rose?"

"I'm fine, Mama."

Mr. Frontier strode in, his spurs jingling, his Stetson in his hand. His brow was furrowed, his expression humble.

Oliver followed behind, his eyes behind his glasses dancing with questions.

Mr. Frontier's gaze went from Zane to Mrs. Taylor to Rose. Then he cleared his throat. "I have several apologies to make," he said as he twisted the Stetson in his hand, and for a moment, he reminded Rose of Oliver.

"I failed you all. Pearson kept plaguing me about the show closing. It was all I could think about. The Wild West is my life!" His voice rose dramatically, but then he smiled sheepishly. "However, that's no excuse. Zane, I knew you didn't shoot Judson. Only I was too preoccupied to doubt Pearson when he said he'd gotten you a lawyer. And Mary Hannah,"—Mr. Frontier turned toward Rose's mama—"I put the show's needs before your family's. I'm sorry."

"I accept your apology, Mr. Frontier," she said.

"And, Rose, I am guilty of not listening to you. You alone unmasked Pearson as a scoundrel and a thief. If you hadn't acted so bravely, he would have shot Senator North and gotten away."

"It wasn't only me," Rose protested. "I couldn't have done it alone. Not only did the Sioux capture Mr. Pearson, but White Bear helped me focus my thoughts. I suspected Mr. Pearson, only I couldn't figure out how he could have stolen Zane's revolver at the same time that he was announcing the show."

Mr. Frontier's bushy brows rose. "That is an interesting dilemma."

"With White Bear's help, I thought back to the night General Judson was shot, and I realized that Mr. Pearson *didn't* announce the entrance of the Dry Gulch Stage."

"I get it now." Oliver pushed up his glasses. "He was off stealing Zane's Colt!"

"That's right. Remember how we pondered that, Oliver?" Rose asked.

Mr. Frontier stared at them as if incredulous. "By golly, you're right!" He slapped his Stetson against his leg. "That night I wondered what happened to Pearson's announcement. Then, in all the confusion, it clean left my mind. Thank you, Rose, for figuring it out."

"Your son helped me." Rose looked from Mr. Frontier to Oliver.

Putting his arm around Oliver, Mr. Frontier hugged his son.

Zane chuckled. "I never would have figured it out, either. I was too busy wooing Abigail behind the grandstand."

"I'm sure her father was delighted to hear that," Mama said primly, and Rose and Oliver giggled.

"Now should we let the journalists in?" Mr. Frontier asked, directing his question to Mama.

She smoothed Rose's hair off her forehead. "I think we'll let them wait until tomorrow."

Rose pulled the quilt up to her chin. "Journalists?" she repeated.

Mr. Frontier grinned. "Seems they're hot to interview

Trick-Riding Rose, who thrilled tonight's audience with
her daring feats."

Trick-Riding Rose? Zane had called her that only days
before. Rose hesitated, wondering if Mr. Frontier was
just joshing.

"The newspapermen have already named you," Zane
said. "With a little help from someone," he added, trying
but failing to look innocent.

"Wh-what are you saying?" Rose stammered.

Mr. Frontier propped one hand on his hip. "I'm asking
if you can handle your own act, Miss Rose."

"You're serious?" She could barely choke out the words.
He nodded.

"Mama?" Rose held her breath, waiting for her to
say no.

Mama smiled. "I can't hold you back any longer, Rose
Hannah. Zane assures me you're the best rider in Kentucky.
Of course, you're going to have to quit getting shot at.
And" — Mama said *and* so sternly that Rose knew her
consent was too good to be true — *"And* you're going to
have to wear a proper outfit." Reaching behind her, she
held up a fringed riding jacket and skirt made of the soft-
est cream-colored suede. "I'd been working on this little
by little. I guess now's the right time for you to have it."

Rose gasped. "Why, it's beautiful!"

"And look, Rose." Oliver took the skirt and held it
toward her. "It's like that bicycling outfit we saw in the

magazine. With the split skirt." He puffed out his chest. "I showed the picture to your mama."

"Oliver did indeed help me finish your skirt," Mama confirmed. "We decided it would be much safer than your dress flying everywhere, threatening to catch on your saddle horn. Besides, Oliver assured me that split skirts will soon be worn by modern women everywhere."

Zane shook his head. "What scandalous wear will ladies think up next?"

Rose held the skirt to her cheek. She recognized the suede she'd seen on the sewing machine. All this time, Mama had been working on an outfit for *her*, not for Mr. Frontier or Zane.

She sniffed back tears. "Why, it's perfect, Mama. And Oliver. Thank you."

"Then it's settled," Mr. Frontier said. "Rose, as soon as you're mended, we're putting your act on the posters and advertisements." He waved his hand in an arc. "*Trick-Riding Rose.* If tonight was a sample, you'll be a hit!"

CHAPTER 15

TRICK-RIDING ROSE

"Mama, I just want to try it on," Rose declared the next morning. She was perched on the edge of the cot dressed only in her chemise, her suede riding outfit in her lap. Mama sat beside her, combing out Rose's tangled hair.

"The doctor said to rest today, Rose Hannah. That means nothing strenuous until Oliver comes for your studies."

Studies! Rose made a face. Being trapped inside the tent with multiplication problems and geography would prove more painful than her wound.

"He didn't say I couldn't dress," Rose protested. "It's not like I'm going to run outside and ride Raven."

"Oh, all right." Mama set the comb on the cot and picked up the jacket. "I'm curious myself how it will fit. Now slip the sleeve carefully over your bandage."

Breathless, Rose slipped her arms into the jacket.

The suede was so soft and fine, it felt like silk against her skin. "Oh, Mama. It's perfect!"

"Here, let me button it. I don't want you to hurt your shoulder." Mama smiled as if pleased. "It's kind of nice to fuss over you again, Rose Hannah."

Rose grinned back. "It's kind of nice to be fussed over." She held up her left arm so the fringe dangled from the wrist-length sleeve. Tiny bone buttons marched evenly down the front of the bodice, which hugged her waist. A stripe of darker suede accented the collar.

"It fits just right. Now the skirt." She jumped off the cot. "I can't wait to try it."

Mama bent over and helped Rose step into the skirt. When Rose pulled it up, it felt odd, like men's pants, except that the gathered material was full and fell below her knees. But then she bent her limbs as though straddling a horse, and a grin broke over her face. "It's just right for riding. No loose material flapping in the wind."

Mama's cheeks colored. "I don't know. I do believe it's immodest. You'll be the talk of every town."

"I know I will, Mama." Rose strutted across the tent, her hands on her hips. "But, I promise, they'll be talking about my riding, not my clothes! Where's Zane? I want him to see it."

"Zane's practicing his shooting act. Tonight's going to be another sell-out show."

Rose stopped in her tracks. "Who's assisting him?"

Mama hid a grin. "Miss Abigail Reed, I believe. Not that she'll take over for you. Zane just thought that since your arm was hurt, you might need help tonight. So he's instructing Miss Abigail on how to set up the targets and spring the trap."

Rose snorted. "I doubt that's all he's teaching her."

"Rose Hannah, mind your thoughts."

"Mrs. Taylor?" a voice called from the front of the tent.

Rose turned. It was Alma's husband.

Mama stood up. "Yes, Mr. Nelson?"

"It's my wife. She's asking for you."

"Tell your wife I'll be right there." Mama grabbed her shawl from the clothes tree. "Now you wait right here, Rose. Oliver should be along any minute. Change out of your riding outfit and find your slate. You're not too weak to practice your multiplication tables."

"Yes, ma'am," Rose said.

As soon as Mama left, Rose peeked outside the tent. She had no intention of practicing multiplication. She had to try out her new outfit. Even more important, she had to thank White Bear. Without the chief's help, she never would have saved Senator North and freed Zane.

When she was sure that Mama was out of sight, Rose sneaked off in the other direction. Her shoulder and ribs ached, but it was no worse than other tumbles she'd taken off a horse.

She was rounding the corner of the headquarters tent

when she ran smack into Oliver. Flushing, Oliver jumped
backward. His glasses hung crooked off his nose.

"Rose, are you hurt? I didn't see you. Is your shoulder
all right?"

"Blast my shoulder, Oliver," Rose grumbled. "You got
my new outfit dirty!" She brushed off the suede skirt.

Oliver whistled. "It looks real pretty."

Rose's mouth fell open. "Oliver! You whistled!"

"By golly, I did!" He grinned proudly. "Who knows,
I just might try riding a horse next."

Rose glanced shyly at him. "You know, Oliver, it's
all right by me if you don't ever ride a horse. I like you—
city ways and all."

Oliver's face turned beet red. Reaching up, Rose
righted his glasses. "See you for studies," she said, adding
as she turned away, "I'll be late. Start without me."

"Where are you going?"

"To thank White Bear."

"What'll I tell your mama?"

"Don't tell her anything. Tell her you don't know where
I went."

He blinked. "But how can I tell her I don't know where
you went when I *do* know where you went?"

"*Oliver!*" Rose exclaimed, exasperated.

He gave her a lopsided grin, and she laughed as she
ran lickety-split to the Sioux camp. When she got there,
she skidded to a halt. In the middle of the ring of tipis,

White Bear sat stiffly in a high-backed chair while around him his sons put out their fires and packed their gear.

Slowly, Rose walked toward him. She knew there was another show tonight. Why were the Sioux leaving?

"White Bear?" Rose couldn't wait for him to address her first. "What's happening?"

"It is time to go home."

Rose stared at him. "Home?" she repeated, confused. Home for her was the Wild West show. It took her a minute to remember that White Bear's home was in South Dakota.

He nodded, his eyes intent on the goings-on around him. "I am tired of the noise. Tired of crowds. I need to be back on the plains. Back with my people."

Rose crouched beside the chair. A lump rose in her throat. She swallowed hard, trying to keep from crying in front of the chief.

"I'll miss you," she choked out.

White Bear laid his palm on her head. "I need to go home and lead my people. I cannot ignore white men and their laws any longer. My people need me to protect our land."

Rose nodded. "I understand. And—and I want to thank you. You were the only one who would help me. You knew the truth about Pearson, and you helped me see it." Huge tears rolled down her cheeks.

White Bear was quiet for a moment before he spoke.

"I have a gift for you." He nodded over her head. Rose wiped her eyes with the back of her hand, then looked over her shoulder. One Feather was leading Swift Raven from the stable yard.

Rose's jaw dropped. Slowly, she stood up.

"Swift Raven will help you remember us. And he'll keep you safe while you ride like a warrior."

"Thank you!" She gasped as One Feather handed her Raven's lead rope. "I've never had such a wonderful gift!" She stroked the pony's velvety black muzzle, the tears still streaming down her cheeks. "But, White Bear, I don't have a gift for you."

He put his fist against his heart. "Your gift is here. You remind me that not all white people are like Judson and Pearson."

Crying harder, Rose turned and hugged the chief. He touched her shoulder and said, "Ride now, Rose. Ride like a Sioux."

Snuffling back her tears, she nodded. She grabbed a hunk of Raven's mane and leaped onto the pony's back, ignoring the pain in her shoulder. Her legs hugged his sides. Her skirt worked! Now she'd ride even *better* than the cowboys and *vaqueros*.

White Bear smacked Raven's rump and the pony took off. Rose and Raven cantered past the tipis and cold campfires and onto the empty track.

The wind blew against Rose's cheeks, drying her tears.

She could feel Raven's strong muscles beneath her as they galloped toward the grandstand.

Warrior and horse, moving as one. Rose heard White Bear's deep voice, and she knew she'd never forget her friend.

When they passed the grandstand, Rose imagined herself waving to the audience as she finished her act with the Warrior Stand. She felt a surge of joy, and for the first time in days her heart felt wild and free.

Zane was safe, the Wild West was playing on, Raven was hers to ride forever, and her dream had come true.

Trick-Riding Rose.

She smiled at the wonderful sound of it.

1886

A Peek into the Past

LOOKING BACK: 1886

Colorful posters drew huge audiences to Buffalo Bill's Wild West show.

Sharpshooting cowboys, stampeding buffalo, masked bandits, a great Sioux leader, and "Little Sure Shot" Annie Oakley— these were all attractions of real Wild West shows, which thrilled audiences in 1886.

The show Rose performs in is based on the most famous Wild West show of all—Buffalo Bill's. Like Levi Frontier, William Cody (Buffalo Bill) was a colorful character. Before becoming a

William Cody, better known as Buffalo Bill

showman, he was an army scout, wilderness guide, and buffalo hunter. His real-life adventures captured the attention of folks living in the East, who loved tales of the "wild and woolly West." Cody was featured in dime novels, plays, and newspaper articles. But his greatest fame began with the first Wild West exhibition in 1883.

Cody promoted the show as "an exact reproduction of fierce frontier life." His "outdoor extravaganza" was full of noise, color, and drama. A 20-piece band played throughout the show. A booming-voiced

Buffalo Bill's cowboy band

announcer introduced one action-packed act after another: whooping Indians in war paint attacking a settler's cabin, galloping Pony Express riders, sharpshooters firing pistols and rifles, hunters chasing buffalo, cowboys wrangling longhorns, and trick riders performing amazing feats on horseback.

Wild West riders galloping into their act

Audiences loved it all. In 1885 alone, Buffalo Bill's show played to an estimated 1 million people in more than 40 cities in the United States and Canada. In 1887, the show traveled to England and performed for Queen Victoria's Golden Jubilee.

Buffalo Bill's Wild West toured America and Europe for almost 30 years, helping to create the popular myth of frontier life that still lives on today. Wild West

A Colt revolver in its gun box, and glass balls used as sharpshooting targets

shows never presented Indians living peacefully in families and communities, or settlers farming and starting towns. Instead, Buffalo Bill's Wild West was full of sharpshooting white men, fierce Indians, and wild animals.

At first, females in the show could play only pioneer women who needed rescuing or Indian women doing camp chores. No female performers were mentioned on posters or programs. Then, in 1885, Cody hired Annie Oakley. Born in Ohio, Annie—whose real name was Phoebe Anne Moses—learned to hunt with a rifle to feed her family. At age 15, she won a shooting contest against Frank Butler, a marksman who could "shoot the flame off a candle." A year later, she married him and adopted the name Annie Oakley. They became "Butler and

Sharpshooter Annie Oakley

Oakley," partners on stage—but Annie attracted all the attention. Audiences were used to seeing male sharpshooters—not a five-foot, 100-pound woman shooting coins out of a man's hand and then blowing kisses to the audience! When Annie joined the Wild West, her act became an instant hit.

At first, newspapers criticized Oakley for competing and *winning* in a male sport and flaunting herself before audiences. At that time, the only females who made a living from

A trick rider spins a lasso while hanging from her horse by one leg.

sports were lady wrestlers and circus acrobats, not respectable women. But Oakley's act was so popular that Buffalo Bill soon hired more female performers. Several rode bucking broncs, and one, Emma Lake Hickock, was a trick rider like Rose.

In 1886, however, audiences would have been shocked to see Rose wearing her split skirt. "Divided garments" weren't fully accepted until the 1920s. Before then, a proper lady rode sidesaddle wearing a long skirt. In 1895, Montana rancher Evelyn Cameron wrote that when she wore her split skirt into town, "a warning was given to me to abstain from riding in the streets of Miles City lest I be arrested!"

A fancy leather riding skirt made about 1910

Like the Sioux in Rose's story, Native Americans appeared extensively in Wild West shows. By the mid-1880s, the Indian wars were over and most tribes had been forced onto reservations. Each spring and fall, showmen like Buffalo Bill went to western reservations to hire Indians for their shows. During these "sign-up" days, hundreds of Native Americans arrived in their finest dress, hoping to be chosen.

Show life required Indians to travel far from their homes and face the jeers of white audiences. But performing was one of the few ways that Indians could make money, and traveling with a Wild West troupe often gave them more freedom than they had on reservations.

Native Americans played many roles in Wild West shows. They performed ceremonial dances, shot with bows and arrows, rode bareback, and re-enacted events such as the Battle of Little Bighorn, where the Sioux, led by Sitting Bull, defeated Custer's troops.

Rose's friend White Bear is modeled after Sitting Bull, one of the last Sioux leaders to surrender to the government. Cody recruited Sitting Bull in 1885. Audiences often booed the Sioux leader when he rode into the arena, but he formed friendships with white performers, including Annie Oakley.

Like White Bear, Sitting Bull was proud, wise, and generous with his money. He was amazed at the poverty he saw in the East

*This image from a Wild West poster features
an Indian performer on his pinto pony.*

and was quoted as saying, "Among Indians, a man who had plenty of food shared it with those who had none. It is unthinkable for an Indian to feed himself while others go hungry within eyesight." The ragged children he saw in cities convinced him that whites would never do anything good for Indian people.

Unfortunately, Sitting Bull's distrust was justified. In 1887, the Dawes Allotment Act became law—despite the opposition of some white people like the fictional Senator North. The Dawes Act aimed to destroy Indians' traditional hunting and gathering way of life by forcing tribes on more than 100 reservations to give up their land. Small plots were then assigned, or "allotted," to individual Indians in an attempt to turn them into farmers. The remaining land was sold at bargain prices to settlers and to land speculators like Mr. Pearson.

The Dawes Act was a disaster for Native Americans. It broke up tribes from the plains to the Pacific. Not only did tribes lose vast expanses of land, but many individuals lost their plots of land to whites as well.

As Red Cloud, Chief of the Oglala Sioux, said about white men, "They made us promises, more than I can remember, but they never kept but one; they promised to take our land, and they took it."

An artist's portrayal of Plains Indian life before whites came to the West

About the Author

Like Rose, Alison Hart practically grew up on horseback. She learned to ride at age five and has been hooked ever since—although she's never tried to trick ride!

Ms. Hart is the author of more than sixty books, many of them about girls and horses. Her novel *Shadow Horse* was nominated for the 2000 Edgar Allan Poe Award for Best Children's Mystery.

Besides writing books, she teaches English and creative writing at Blue Ridge Community College in Virginia. She is also a court-appointed special advocate for abused and neglected children. Pursuing her interest in mysteries and crime investigation, she recently graduated from the Staunton Citizens Police Academy.

She lives in Virginia with her husband, two kids, a guinea pig, two dogs, and three horses. She's still horse-crazy and loves to ride her Quarter Horse, April.